1

'It's not too late; I can always turn around,' Tracy said to herself when the sign announcing the Derbyshire village of Eyam came into view. Just because she had said she'd be here didn't mean she couldn't change her mind. Maybe just another day . . . ?

She hadn't seen her family since the beginning of March, when they had come to London. Tracy knew her mum was upset because she hadn't joined them in Scarborough during the summer, but honestly, she'd been buried in paperwork. There was no way she could have taken four days off, and then another two and a half weeks now. Her boss would have had a fit if she'd even suggested it; as it was, the top brass were none too happy.

But this year, she'd allowed her mother to guilt her into coming home

1

for Christmas. Mum had given the 'we're not getting any younger' speech over the phone, and when that hadn't worked, she'd gone into all the things that Tracy would have to do to make her flat child-proof. The first thing that would have to go would be her ornamental collection of rabbits — it had worked. She hadn't believed how disruptive having a two-year-old around could be. For the sake of her Pendelfin rabbits she gave in.

Tracy left London on the nineteenth of December. She hadn't taken her full holiday allowance in years, and her boss was annoyed that she'd chosen to do so this year — but, decision made, Tracy had refused to disappoint her family. When she'd told her mum she was going to drive home for Christmas instead of using public transport, she'd had to promise not to drive straight through from London to Eyam. Of course, her mother did think she was coming by car — Tracy wasn't looking forward to the confrontation when

DIFFICULT DECISIONS

Tracy Stewart left the Derbyshire village of Eyam to pursue her dream of becoming a solicitor. Returning home for Christmas is the last thing she wants to do. A brush with Mike O'Neill starts to change her mind, but is it enough to make her stay? Mike has taken over running his father's bookshop, whilst working as a writer in secret. But can he keep his secret as well as the girl he loves?

Books by Charlotte McFall
in the Linford Romance Library:

HEALING THE HURT

CHARLOTTE McFALL

DIFFICULT DECISIONS

Complete and Unabridged

LINFORD
Leicester

First published in Great Britain in 2015

First Linford Edition
published 2015

A catalogue record for this book is available
from the British Library.

ISBN 978–1–4448–2406–3

Published by
F. A. Thorpe (Publishing)
Anstey, Leicestershire

Set by Words & Graphics Ltd.
Anstey, Leicestershire
Printed and bound in Great Britain by
T. J. International Ltd., Padstow, Cornwall

This book is printed on acid-free paper

Mum realised she'd ridden the bike up. She'd stretched her journey not only to satisfy her mother, but also to add to the pleasure of the ride. She'd made it a two-day journey, visiting friends on the way, even though she could easily have got to Eyam in a few hours.

As much as she was looking forward to seeing her family, she'd have much preferred to spend her entire Christmas holiday at a hotel. But her mother would have found her somehow and dragged her home.

She slowed her purple Honda down as she entered the small village. She'd only just got her new toy — it was her Christmas present to herself — and this was its first major trip.

As she cruised along the High Street, scanning the village square decorated for Christmas, she became aware that nothing had really changed in the ten years since she'd been gone. The village's oldest shops, festooned in greenery, lined the sides of the street just as they had years ago when she'd shopped there. While some of them might boast a new coat of paint, for the most part it seemed to her that time had stood still. A huge Christmas tree stood in the park at the end of the street, waiting to be decorated during the Christmas Fair on Sunday. The Christmas lights would be switched on as it grew dark. People were already hard at work erecting the stalls for the event, including the pretend North Pole where children would have one last trip to visit Santa.

As she drove along slowly, she noticed a couple of new shops, including her sister's bakery. The only other shop she really wanted to see was O'Neill's Bookshop. It had been her favourite place in the small village where she'd considered herself an outcast. In O'Neill's, she could escape to new worlds and enjoy wonderful adventures. Reading had been the only thing that got her through her unhappy teen years.

When she saw that it was still there

and still owned by the O'Neill family — at least, according to the sign it was — Tracy pulled her bike into a parking spot across the street from the shop. She turned off the bike and flipped out the kickstand. Removing her helmet, she shook her long hair from side to side and ran her fingers through it in an effort to unflatten it, and pulled the zip down a few inches on the black-and-purple leather armoured jacket she wore for protection. She put her arms out to the side, stretching to ease her aching muscles.

She noticed a number of people looking out of their shop windows. No doubt they'd heard the bike and were curious about the rider. Unless things had changed, a girl dressed in skin-tight leather riding a motorcycle was bound to cause a stir. She smiled and wondered how many of them would realise it was her — probably not too many.

She was proud of the way she'd changed over the years. She wasn't that shy, skinny girl the other children made fun of and the village residents ignored. Tracy smiled wryly. Well, it looked like they were noticing her now.

If she had been recognised, no doubt one of the concerned villagers was on the phone right now, setting her mother straight. Mum probably wouldn't be impressed she'd made a stop in the village instead of coming straight to the house, but what else was new?

Several people on the street were craning their necks, watching her saunter over to O'Neill's Bookshop, her crash helmet hanging casually from her hand the way another woman's handbag might. Someone in the bookshop was looking out of the window, every bit as curious as the others were, but whoever it was quickly stood back as she approached.

Tracy stood on the pavement, admiring her old haunt, and let the past claim her. As she entered, the antique bell above the door tinkled, announcing her arrival just as it had all those years ago. She stopped in the doorway and allowed memories of her hours spent in this place to wash over her. She took a deep breath, absorbing the familiar aroma of old books, a scent she loved. She was suddenly anxious to see Mr. O'Neill again; they'd spent hours together discussing their favourite books.

Tracy thought it strange when no one came to greet her. No matter what he'd been doing, Mr. O'Neill always came at the sound of the bell. Sadness filled her. Perhaps he didn't own it anymore. She supposed it was common practice for new owners to keep a business's original name.

'Hello, is anyone here?' Her voice echoed in the emptiness of the shop.

A touch nervous, she moved deeper into the shop, and started when she heard a man clear his throat. She looked over in the direction of the sound and was pleasantly surprised when a stranger stepped out from between two rows of shelves.

The man was most definitely not the one she'd expected. He wore jeans, a white T-shirt, and a grey-and-black striped jumper. His feet were stuffed into black trainers. He took her breath away. Clean-shaven, with striking green eyes that peered at her from behind large black-framed glasses, he was intelligent-looking — and gorgeous. Even though she never acted on the yearning men like that sometimes evoked in her, she could appreciate a masterpiece when she saw it. His expensive, spicy, tantalizing cologne aroused a sudden desire that pulsed through her. Usually shy around men, she stared at him openly, and felt her cheeks grow hot at the wholly unfamiliar turn her thoughts were taking.

He seemed vaguely familiar, and she rattled her brain trying to place him, but try as she might, she couldn't imagine anyone she knew from back then looking like this today. Surely if she had seen this individual before, she'd have remembered him?

'Can I help you?' He looked at her directly, his gaze taking in every inch of her. The look on his face said he liked what he saw.

'I was looking for the owner, Mr. O'Neill. Is he around?' She was amazed that her voice sounded so normal when her heart was beating so fast he must surely be able to hear it.

'I'm sorry. My dad isn't here right now. Is there something I can do for you?'

Of course! She remembered him now. Mr. O'Neill had had two children, a son and a daughter, both older than she was. Although they'd all gone to the same school, the age gap between them had put his son a couple of years ahead of her. If her memory served correctly, his name was Mike, but he couldn't possibly have looked this gorgeous back then — not that she would have noticed. With her low self-esteem and poor self-image, she'd walked through her teen years with her nose firmly planted in whatever book had captured her attention. Back then, a boy like him would never have given her a second glance.

Slightly disappointed that she wouldn't get to see her old friend after all, she replied, 'Oh! Where is he?'

'My parents are visiting my sister in Ireland at the moment. They travel quite a lot these days.'

She and Mr. O'Neill had spoken for hours about all the places in the world they'd like to see. She'd been too young to travel anywhere but in her books, and the shop had kept Mr. O'Neill's feet firmly planted in Eyam. She was glad he'd had an opportunity to make his dreams come true. She looked at Mike and smiled.

'That's wonderful. I bet he's having a great time. He always said he wanted to travel.'

'You know my father well?' His voice was tinged with curiosity and confusion.

She laughed. 'I certainly used to. I counted him as a really good friend when I was growing up in Eyam. This shop was like my second home.'

'Tracy Stewart? Is that really you?'

She nodded, pleasantly surprised he knew her name. 'Guilty as charged. It's Mike, isn't it?'

'Yes. I heard through the grapevine you'd be home for Christmas; you're a lawyer now, aren't you?' He looked her up and down again.

'Nothing gets by the small village gossips, does it?' Her voice was laced with sarcasm, and she was unable to keep her disdain from coming through. She was sure he noticed her tone, but to his credit he didn't comment.

'Did you want something? Or did you stop by just to see my father?'

'Well, I could do with a new book or two. I can't go without something to read the whole time I'm here. I feel lost without a book on the go.'

She was beginning to feel uncomfortably warm and wasn't sure if the cause was the leather or the man standing in front of her. Needing to cool off, she unzipped her jacket. His eyes followed the gaping zipper teeth as they opened.

'I can help you with that.' His voice was husky.

'Help me with what?' she squeaked.

'Erm . . . a new book, remember? I can help you find one.' He looked amused. 'You did want a book, didn't you? Isn't that what you just said?'

Tracy felt her cheeks heat, embarrassed that he might see how much he'd affected her. Ignoring her discomfort, she fought to maintain her poise.

'Yes! Yes, of course.' She smiled sweetly and sauntered down the aisles of bookshelves, trying desperately to look as if she didn't have a care in the world. She wanted him to admire her, to see how she'd changed. She could feel his eyes on her as she walked away with more than a little sway in her hips. What harm could it do to engage in an innocent bit of flirtation while she was here? In a couple of weeks she'd be back in London, preparing briefs. She was entitled to a little harmless fun, wasn't she? After all, all work and no play wasn't healthy.

'Well, I'll be over here if you need any help.'

'Thanks.' Tracy smiled at him again over her shoulder. She watched as he ran his fingers through his hair and shook his head. She'd definitely had an effect on him — she hoped it was as strong as the one he'd had on her.

* * *

Mike tried to look busy as Tracy browsed the bookshelves. The woman had definitely changed. Though he was two years older than she was, he remembered her from school. Thinking about it, they'd been a lot alike back then, both of them with their noses always stuck in books, not quite fitting in with the rest. The similarities should have made them friends, but as a teen he hadn't had the nerve to talk to a girl, even one as unpopular as himself.

He remembered her coming into the

shop those afternoons when he worked in the back unpacking boxes of new books and sorting them to put on the shelves. He'd been enchanted by her, watching secretly from behind the shelves. How animated she'd become when she'd talked to Dad about the current book she was reading or about the places she'd like to visit. He would stand hidden in the back, just listening to her voice, too shy to even consider joining the discussions. He'd really liked the girl she became when she visited the shop back then — a girl who was nothing like the mouse he saw at school each day.

Somehow, he didn't think unpopularity would be her problem now. She was the perfect woman — obviously intelligent, extremely sexy with or without the leather, and for goodness' sake, she rode a motorcycle! She exuded confidence.

Despite his best efforts, he was having a hard time controlling his body. She was affecting him far more deeply than he'd expected. He took a deep breath, forcefully tore his eyes away from her leather-clad bottom, and returned to sorting the new shipment of books that had just arrived.

It didn't take long for him to become immersed in the jacket blurbs, and he jumped when he heard her shout. Dropping the book he was holding, he pushed his way through the boxes crowding the aisle to see what had upset her.

'What's wrong?' He hurried to her side, worried that she'd hurt herself somehow. It was true that the worst injury you could probably get in a bookshop was a paper cut, but he was concerned all the same.

'I'll tell you what's wrong — you have all of G.L. O'Michael's books shoved back here where no one can see them. Are you mad?'

He laughed at the look of disbelief on her face. 'I take it you're a fan?'

'Of course I'm a fan! Isn't everyone? He's a great author, even though he's the Howard Hughes of writers — a total recluse. How come you have his latest book? It isn't due out for another two weeks.'

He ran his fingers through his hair again, a nervous gesture he made when he was caught off guard. He didn't know how he was going to explain having advance copies of the book on the shelf, and he certainly wasn't about to tell her the truth.

'I know the author; we went to uni together.' The half-lie slid smoothly off his tongue.

'You know G.L. O'Michael?' she asked, doubt evident in her voice.

Oh dear! How could he get out of this?

He turned away from her, trying to think of a way out of the quicksand into which he'd inadvertently stepped. He wasn't about to share his secret with a virtual stranger, but he was pretty sure she wasn't going to let it go. He needed to come up with something quickly — something believable that wouldn't get him into any more trouble.

'G.L. sends me advance copies of his books when his publisher gives him the go-ahead. I'm technically not supposed to put them on display yet, so don't go broadcasting it.'

'Who would I tell?' The look on her face told him she thought he was being ridiculous.

'I don't know; maybe your lawyer friends in London.' He'd put a little more heat into his voice than he'd needed, but he was dying here, sinking deeper and deeper by the minute.

He watched her roll her eyes. 'Let me get right on that. I'll tell them to drop everything and come to Eyam to buy a book they'll be able to pick up at home in a matter of days.'

'Yes, well, maybe my comment was a little over the top, but there is the legal aspect to consider. Plus, if you're a fan, you know he doesn't like the spotlight. He plays his cards close to his chest. I'm a little protective of him.'

She laughed. 'A little protective?

There are she-bears in the woods that could take lessons from you.' She shook her head. 'This is going to drive me insane — knowing you know the man who writes these addictive books, and won't tell me who he is — but I'll let it go. For now!'

He exhaled and relaxed. He'd take the temporary reprieve. He was fairly certain that she'd ferret out the truth soon enough, but he wasn't ready for it to be sooner rather than later.

He watched her as she selected her books, including the one not yet released.

She looked at him and grinned. 'Getting to read Book Four early will do for now, but I'll be back. When I am, I'll get you to tell me all about the talented man behind my favourite character, Detective Rick Foster.'

The idea he'd see her again, even if it were only for her to pry information out of him, pleased him more than he expected it to.

'Maybe I can even convince you to

get these books signed for me,' she continued, batting her eyelashes and smiling sweetly.

'I'll see what I can do.' He smiled. 'Got everything you want?'

Instead of answering straight away, she stood there looking at him as if she could somehow see into his soul. He wondered nervously what was running through her head.

At last, she nodded and preceded him to the counter where the till stood. He scanned the books, added up the price, and placed her purchases in a bag.

'Thanks, Mike. I'll see you soon.' She accepted the package and prepared to leave.

'Come back anytime.' He was surprised by how much he meant the words. He had a feeling that life around Tracy Stewart would never be dull.

He stood in the shop window, watching her cross the street to her bike. Once there, she secured the bag, donned her helmet, and threw her leg over the seat. The bike started smoothly. She glanced back towards the shop, as if she knew he was watching her, and eased her bike into the flow of traffic and away.

2

Tracy pulled her bike into the driveway of her childhood home, turning off the engine. Looking up, she realised she'd missed the old house, but she still doubted the wisdom of coming here for a two-week stay. She avoided looking towards the porch, decorated in greenery and icicle lights, knowing exactly what awaited her.

She was sure someone had notified her mother of her arrival by now, and she'd be standing there, arms crossed, visibly upset for two reasons — the first because Tracy hadn't come straight home, the second because she'd ridden her bike up. She fully expected her mother to tear a strip off her, and she wasn't looking forward to it!

She got off the bike, took the books out of her box, and added them to her rucksack. Removing her helmet, she walked towards her old home, bracing herself for the inevitable.

'You lied to me,' her mother exclaimed, opening the front door. 'You said you were driving home; you didn't say you were riding that death trap here.'

Tracy took a calming breath. Her mum was being overly protective. Sooner or later she would have to come to terms with the fact that Tracy was an adult, entitled to make her own decisions as she saw fit. But right now, arguing wouldn't help; it was better to grin and bear it.

'Hi, Mum. Nice to see you too,' she said sweetly. 'I knew you'd worry more if I told you I'd decided to take the bike instead of the car. I didn't lie — I just withheld some information.' She took the steps slowly, almost reluctantly.

'If you had told me you were coming home on that, I wouldn't have slept a wink. I hate those things.' Her mother stared menacingly at the 'death trap', as she called the motorbike, obviously fighting the urge to go and kick it.

Helmet in hand, Tracy took her mum into her arms and gave her a tight hug. 'I know you hate the fact that I ride, but I love it. The trip here was lovely; there's nothing like the freedom of riding into the wind, Mum. I wish I could make you understand. I did stop overnight along the way though, just as I promised,' she reassured her, spreading her arms so her mother could get a good look at her standing there, and smiled. 'See? Safe and sound!'

Her mother, obviously fighting to keep a welcoming smile off her face, glared at her. 'I don't want to get a call some night from the police telling me they had to scrape you off the pavement somewhere.'

'You won't. I'm careful, really I am.' Time for a change of subject. 'I see toys, indicating the presence of a child nearby.' She pointed to the Wendy house with a doll's pram parked beside it. 'Where's my niece?'

The motorbike was forgotten as soon

as the only grandchild was mentioned, and her mother instead became intent on showing off her pride and joy. Tracy relaxed. The lecture hadn't been as bad as she'd expected.

'Carrie's grown so much since you last saw her, and she's so clever. You should hear her talk! Pictures don't do her justice; wait until you see her. She's an angel! Susan got off a bit early today, and she's just getting her cleaned up.'

Tracy followed her mother into the house, as anxious to see her niece again as her mother was to show her off.

'Susan! Henry! Tracy's home,' her mother called loudly, as if they wouldn't have heard the bike roll up to the house. She'd bet her last penny her father had gone into hiding the second he'd heard her arrive, wanting to avoid her mother's tirade.

She heard her sister cheer with delight from upstairs. 'We'll be down in a minute.'

Her father came out of the kitchen, a huge welcoming smile on his face. Her heart leapt with joy. She was definitely a Daddy's girl.

He opened his arms and she pulled her rucksack from her shoulders, dropped it onto the floor next to her helmet, and ran to him. He wrapped her in a warm hug.

'Hi, Dad. I've missed you.'

'We've missed you too. Welcome home.' He held her close. She smelled the aftershave he'd always used — the scent she associated with him and unwavering love. For the first time since leaving London, she was truly glad she'd decided to come home.

'Let me look at you.' He pushed her an arm's length away from him. His eyebrows lifted quizzically as he took in the tight leather suit she was wearing. He whistled. 'Nice outfit. It's too bad they didn't have one small enough for you.'

She laughed at his ironic comment. 'It's for protection, silly. It has to fit snugly on the bike.'

'Hmm . . . '

Her mother commented on her outfit as well.

'My daughter, a leathers-wearing, bike-riding woman who never comes home. What happened to the girl I raised?' She threw her hands up in the air as if she was the long-suffering wronged party.

Tracy looked deeply into her dad's eyes. 'She grew up.' She noticed he looked a little thinner than he had the last time she'd seen him. Probably jumped on the fitness bandwagon, she thought, dismissing it from her mind.

'Humph!' her mother snorted, picking up the discarded bag from the floor.

'Yes, she most certainly did,' agreed her father. He smiled.

'What have you got in here this time, Tracy?'

She cringed. She was in for another blast. 'Just a few books.'

'Mrs. Harper called me saying she thought she saw you go into O'Neill's, but I told her that was impossible. I told her you'd come straight home when you reached the village; apparently I was wrong. You'd rather go to that bookshop than see your family.'

'Nancy, you asked where the girl you raised was; obviously she's right here, if she stopped at the bookshop before she came home.'

Tracy was surprised to hear her mother chuckle at her father's remark.

'You're right.' She shook her head. She handed Tracy the discarded bag and put the helmet on the table.

The sound of footsteps hurrying down the stairs filled the room. Susan had always been the beautiful one and that hadn't changed. If strangers saw them together, they'd probably never realise they were sisters. Susan was blonde with blue eyes, a long, lean body, and a bubbly personality. People noticed her. When she smiled, she lit up the room. Tracy, on the other hand, had brown wavy hair that rarely co-operated, flashing hazel eyes, and was short and curvy. Quieter and more serious than Susan, she loved her sister more than words could say. While she might hate the fact that Susan showed no evidence of having given birth two years ago — something she knew wouldn't happen if she ever became a mother — she was truly happy to see her. And she couldn't wait to get a better look at the short person who'd buried her face in her mother's trouser leg.

Susan smiled as she disengaged the child and picked her up. 'Come and say hello to Aunty Tracy. I'm sorry it took us so long to get down here, but I didn't want you to see her covered in muck.' Susan laughed; motherhood suited her. She looked happy, maybe a little tired, but Tracy assumed that came with the territory. A two-year-old and running your own business would keep you on your toes. A pang of envy speared her.

'Remember me?' she asked, smiling at the child.

'Aunty Tracy,' Carrie cried and

almost jumped out of her mother's arms.

'Wow,' said Tracy through the lump in her throat. 'You've grown so big! Come and give me a hug and tell me all your news.'

'She'll talk your ear off, Tracy, if you let her,' Susan said with a grin. 'She's got us all wrapped around her little finger, and dancing to her tune.'

'And you love it,' Tracy chuckled. She could see her family's adoration in the way all the attention was now focused on the child squirming to be put down.

'Aunty Tracy, read me a story?' Carrie asked.

Her mum laughed. 'She's almost as big a bookworm as you.'

'Let me get my leathers off and I'll read to you. Go and get your favourite books.' Carrie hurried back upstairs.

Tracy quickly removed her leathers and went into the kitchen to wash her hands, anxious to sit with Carrie. She'd changed so much in nine months, and Tracy was sad to have missed it all. After drying her hands, she went into the living room.

Susan was seated on the leather sofa, a new addition to the room's décor.

'You're lucky,' she said. 'She's only chosen six.'

'Gimme, gimme,' Tracy cried, reaching for the books, making her sister and her niece laugh.

Susan stood and Tracy took her place on the sofa. Carrie immediately climbed onto her lap.

'I brought my best books.' She proudly handed them to Tracy.

'These are some of my favourites too.' The books brought back the bittersweet memories of childhood. She looked up at her sister.

'I've said it before — she's beautiful, Susan. You're doing a great job.'

Her sister nodded, and Tracy knew she was pleased with the praise. 'Thank you; she is wonderful, isn't she?'

'Yes, and she looks just like you,'

Tracy chuckled. She noticed a momentary look of sadness cross her sister's face and wondered what she'd said to affect her sister's mood, but the look was gone almost as quickly as it had appeared. Susan smiled at her.

'If it's alright with you, I'm going to grab a shower before dinner while you're reading. It's a luxury I rarely get these days.'

'It's fine; take all the time you need. We'll be here,' answered Tracy, captivated by the prospect of reading books she hadn't seen in years.

'But you must be tired after your journey. Don't you want to take a shower yourself?'

'I can sleep and shower later. At the moment I'm busy entertaining my niece. Go!'

Susan kissed her on the cheek. 'Okay, I'm going. Yell if you need me.'

She waved off her sister. She and Carrie were going to be just fine.

★　★　★

Mike heard the bike coming along the street before he saw it. He hadn't been able to stop thinking about Tracy ever since she'd come into the shop yesterday. He wasn't sure whether he wanted to see her or not, but when he saw her get off the bike and remove her helmet his mind was made up for him. She bent and shook out her long brown hair. The sun made the highlights in it shimmer like gold. She raised her head and smiled.

Each time he thought about her, his body went on high alert, and if the dreams he'd had last night were anything to go by, things could get interesting between them. He watched her as she made her way through the few cars that were driving down the High Street. One honked his horn at her and she childishly stuck her tongue out at the driver. Mike was still laughing when he opened the door for her.

'Classy,' he remarked as she stepped into the shop.

'I try,' she replied, shrugging her shoulders. 'I'm sure Mum'll get a call any minute complaining about my outrageous behavior.'

'She probably will,' he agreed, knowing how quickly gossip travelled in their small village. It was the main reason he kept his pseudonym secret.

'How's the book business treating you?' she asked, walking over to the counter and leaning against it.

'Very well, and we're doing better every day. E-books have changed the way people read, and small bookshops like this one have to move with the times.' Mike warmed to his theme. 'E-books are the way of the future; they're a great way to protect the environment too. You know, Dad thought about shutting the shop down so he and Mum could travel. I hated the thought of that, so I moved back home a few years ago and took over the management of the shop.'

'You don't mind being back in a small village like Eyam after living in places like Edinburgh and London?'

'How did you know where I'd lived?' He watched as her cheeks began to redden. Blushing women, especially when they were as outgoing and confident as she appeared to be, were a novelty. Now he was really curious.

'My sister told me last night,' she admitted reluctantly.

He smiled. 'You talked about me with your sister? Should I be flattered?' He liked the fact that she was curious enough to ask about him — as long as she didn't get too curious!

'I asked her if she'd ever heard you talk about G.L. O'Michael. I told you I'd find out all about him, and since you wouldn't talk . . . '

He hoped the disappointment didn't show on his face. After all, she had vowed to find out what he knew about her favourite author. He couldn't help but wish she'd been asking about him though!

'And?'

'And she said you don't really talk

too much about anything, even when you go into the bakery for coffee. She said you're the strong silent type, and you tend to keep to yourself. Honestly, I can't see how that works — you're gorgeous! What's wrong with the women of Eyam?'

It was his turn to be embarrassed. It wasn't often that a woman, especially one as striking as she was, spoke to him so directly. It was one more thing he liked about her. In fact, there was no denying it — he fancied her!

He hadn't ever really gone out with any of the women in the village. When he'd first returned to Eyam, all the girls who wouldn't have given him the time of day in school were suddenly interested in him, even some of the married ones, and that had irritated him beyond measure. He hadn't changed, so why the sudden interest now? He enjoyed female company as much as the next man, but made the decision then and there that the women of Eyam were not for him. It wasn't that he didn't want to make a commitment; he simply hadn't found the right girl. For Tracy, though, he might make an exception.

He stood there drinking in the sight of her, dressed in her ripped jeans and tight, long sleeved T-shirt. The woman was stunning, there was no doubt about it; but was he ready to pursue a relationship with someone who had connections to Eyam? When she smiled at him, he suspected he'd been staring at her, probably with that starving puppy look on his face, the one he'd seen on other men's faces over the years. He knew it was a bad idea to even consider the possibility of anything happening with her — apart from anything else, she was going back to London in a couple of weeks — but he could no more stop himself from thinking of the possibility than he could stop breathing. She made the decision for him.

'Do you want to have a drink or coffee with me later, perhaps?' she asked, a little of that teenage self-consciousness evident in her voice, and he was lost.

Unease forgotten, he found himself saying yes.

'Great. What time do you close?'

'Five, as always. Would you like to have dinner?' What was he doing? How had he gone from thinking that a date with her might be a bad idea to asking her to have dinner with him?

'I wish I could, but if I tell my mum I won't be home for tea on my second night here, she'll have a fit. How about I give you a call after we've eaten, when Mum's finished trying to figure out what she did wrong raising me? And making sure my sister doesn't repeat the mistake with my niece, Carrie.' She laughed ruefully.

'Sounds good.' He walked over to the counter where she'd been leaning.

He could have stepped around her to grab a pen and paper, but instead he found himself leaning over her, pressing his body against hers. He heard her breath catch and, standing flush against her like this, he could feel her heart quicken. He reached for a notepad and pen, holding her there momentarily, enjoying the feeling of her body pressed against his. It was only for a second, the time it took to jot down a mobile number, but when he stepped away from her he saw she was slightly flushed. He handed her the piece of paper with his number on.

'Thanks.' She laughed, breaking the spell, and shook her head.

He could tell from her shining eyes that she was enjoying this minor flirtation. He was too.

She put the piece of paper with his mobile number on it into her pocket and moved towards the door. 'See you tonight.'

'I'm looking forward to it.' He smiled, watching her walk away from him and out of the door, seemingly unaware of the alluring sway of her hips.

3

As soon as she passed the edge of the village, Tracy pulled her bike over to the side of the road. Her latest encounter with Mike had left butterflies in her stomach, fluttering madly. Her mind was everywhere except on her riding. She felt as if she were swimming underwater and couldn't come up for air. She put the kickstand down and got off the bike. Pacing helped her think clearly. She'd worn a path in the rug in her office to prove it. She began to walk up and down the side of the road near her bike, trying to make sense of things.

What was happening to her? Over the years she'd become confident and wasn't afraid to go after what she wanted, but she'd never been this brazen with a man. There was something about Mike that drew her, like a moth to a flame, and she found him impossible to resist.

What the hell was she doing? Was it because she was back in Eyam? Was she trying to prove that she wasn't the shy little girl she used to be? Tracy couldn't think straight. Suddenly, she wasn't sure anymore who she was or what she wanted, and it scared the living daylights out of her.

She'd deliberately gone to the bookshop that afternoon to pump Mike for more information about G.L. O'Michael. The fact he knew the reclusive author had her intrigued. She'd wondered briefly if G.L. had used the name 'O'Michael' as a way of honouring his old friend. If they were that close, though, it would be hard to get Mike to give up any information about the man.

Her plan had derailed the moment she'd walked into the bookshop. Mike had looked even sexier and more appealing than he had yesterday. All thoughts of the author flew out of her head. Instead she'd flirted with him, told him to his face that he was gorgeous and, completely at the mercy of her hormones, invited him out for coffee. And he'd accepted!

What was she thinking? The last thing Tracy wanted to do was get involved with someone from Eyam! She hated it here and had no intention of ever coming back again, whereas Mike seemed happy living in this village; he'd come back on purpose. She couldn't possibly imagine why he wanted to live here, of all places, but she did know that, other than being able to spend quality time with her family, this was the last place on earth she wanted to be. Getting involved with Mike was definitely a bad idea.

She'd spend the Christmas holidays here, but once they were over she'd never come back. Next year Carrie would be older and Christmas could be spent in London, the way it had been for the last ten years. She could even foot the bill for a trip away somewhere, if it meant not having to be in Eyam.

She had loads of money in her bank account, and other than paying the rent on her flat and buying clothes, she spent very little of it on anything else. Her largest expense this year had been her bike. Paying for a family holiday might be worth it.

The more she thought about it, the more she considered it would be wise to rescind her invitation, but something about that idea bothered her. Unwilling to admit that Mike did things to her equilibrium no one else ever had, she rationalised that keeping the date would be the only polite thing to do. Besides, if she didn't, how else would she learn more about her favourite author? She brushed aside the fact that thoughts of the author had gone right out the window when she'd laid eyes on Mike's handsome face.

'Whatever!' she said aloud, annoyed when the little voice inside her head laughed at her.

She jumped back on the bike and sped home, putting distance between herself and this man who had her acting in the strangest way.

★ ★ ★

When Tracy opened the door, she saw that her mother had been busy putting the final touches on her Christmas wonderland. The house was decorated more or less the way she remembered it from childhood. Santas of various sizes, shapes and styles posed in corners, wreaths hung on the walls, and fake snow, not a flake out of place, lay under the miniature Christmas village that seemed to have grown substantially in size since the last time she'd seen it. A short white wooden fence surrounded the village, no doubt to keep curious fingers from playing with the breakable figurines.

Christmas had always been her mother's favourite time of year, and she loved all the glitz and decorations that went with it. When had she bought all this stuff and where had she kept it?

Her parents had come to London for Christmas these last ten years, and none of this had come with them. Tracy noticed a number of familiar items as she moved through the house, but there were several new things too. A wave of guilt flooded her. What a sacrifice it must have been for her mother to leave everything behind for the sterile confines of Tracy's flat each year. A fake tree with pitiful decorations didn't stand a chance against all this.

She stared at the only empty spot in the room, knowing that it was where the tree — a real pine, not an artificial one — would stand. On Christmas Eve the whole family would gather to decorate it together. It was a Stewart tradition, the only one she'd continued in London, but it hadn't been the same. Pine-scented spray just couldn't compete with the natural aroma.

When she'd been a child, once the tree had been decorated, they'd all gather in the kitchen to bake and ice buns. Afterwards her father would sit down to read *A Christmas Carol* until she and her sister, buried in a mountain of blankets and pillows on the floor, fell asleep. That particular tradition, the one nearest and dearest to her heart, was one she hoped she could persuade her father to revive this year.

How could she have forgotten all this?

Realising what she'd selfishly ignored over the last few years, Tracy understood why her mum had been adamant she come home for the first Christmas Carrie would remember: she wanted her granddaughter to experience a traditional Stewart Christmas, with all the bells and whistles. She stood there, allowing the memories to wash over her. When they changed to images of future Christmases including Carrie, she knew she couldn't ask the family to give this up. She couldn't deprive her beautiful niece of the chance to make the sort of memories she herself cherished. Since Susan was a single parent — her sister had always adamantly refused to disclose who Carrie's father was — they were all the family Carrie had. Personally, Tracy disagreed with Susan's insistence that Carrie's father never learn of her existence, and she planned to have a heart-to-heart talk with her before the Christmas break was over.

Tracy spotted the ugly robin she'd made in reception class and couldn't believe her mother had kept it all these years. She picked up the fragile decoration and shook her head. Her mother had placed it in the same spot it had occupied since the day Tracy had brought it home. Her mum had made such a fuss about it and had displayed it so that everyone who came into the house could see how talented her daughter was.

Tracy smiled at the memory, and was ashamed of how self-centred she'd been all these years. Putting the robin back where it belonged, she moved deeper into the house, knowing where she'd find her mother at this time of day. She needed to talk to her and apologise for her attitude and behaviour. She'd put her wants and needs above all others. She felt guilty and hoped everyone could forgive her.

She walked towards the kitchen at the back of the house and found her mother standing at the counter preparing tea. Tracy walked over and kissed her on the cheek. There had been tension between them since her arrival home, but at the moment the nostalgia she felt reminded her of how much she loved her mum, regardless of how over-protective and critical she might be.

'Hi, love. Glad you're home in one piece.' Her mother's quip made Tracy smile, and her mum caught it. 'What was that for? Not that I'm complaining.'

'Just because. I told you, the bike is safe; you'll get used to it. Maybe I'll take you out for a ride one of these days.' The look of absolute horror on her mother's face made her laugh.

She watched as her mother prepared the salad that would accompany the homemade lasagna she smelled in the oven. 'Lasagna for tea — my favourite. Where is everyone?'

She'd noticed that Mum's meals had changed since the last time she'd been home. Everything she served now was healthier than before, probably because of Carrie, and that was a good thing. Too much rich food and she wouldn't get into that new trouser suit she'd bought for work. Her stomach grumbled.

'I know it is.' Her mother smiled. 'Your father is in the study, and Susan is playing upstairs with Carrie.'

'The house looks fantastic by the way. You've certainly collected a lot of new decorations since the last time I was here.'

'Thanks. Your father always tells me I go overboard, but you know how much I love Christmas. It'll be nice to have a tree to go with the rest of it this year.'

'Do you want some help with tea?'

She knew the answer was probably no, but she wanted to hold on to this relaxed feeling between her and her mother.

'That's nice of you to ask, but it's almost ready. Why don't you go up and spend time with Susan and Carrie for a while?'

'If you're certain, I will, but I'd like to ask you something first.'

Her mother nodded. Tracy saw her shoulders tense a little, but she didn't stop her preparations.

'How come you all came to London every year for Christmas when you would have enjoyed it so much more at home?'

Her mother smiled. 'That's a silly question. We came to London because you were there. We'd have loved to have you come home, but we knew it would have been hard for you to get away. First, you were at university, and then you were working hard to make a name for yourself. We understood. Being together was more important than where we were. I'm happy you made it home this year, though — even if it was on the back of that death trap.'

Tracy let go of some, but not all, of the guilt she'd felt in the living room. She'd been afraid her family might have resented her, but there was no trace of that in her mother's answer. Instead, she glimpsed the unconditional love her mother and father had always lavished on her. It was time she started putting the needs of others before her own.

'Thanks, Mum.' She pecked her on the cheek and went upstairs to play with her niece and get ready for dinner.

*   *   *

Once the meal was over Tracy supervised Carrie's bath, read two stories, kissed her goodnight, and left her to Susan for their nightly tucking-in ritual. She left mother and daughter together and went to her room to get ready to meet Mike.

She'd been pondering it all through

tea, trying to convince the fluttering in her stomach that it wasn't a date, it was simply a means of getting vital information out of him that he was withholding from her; but the butterflies didn't believe her any more than the little voice in her head.

Earlier, in the comfort of her bedroom, she'd called Mike to see where he'd like to meet. He'd suggested outside the shop, and she'd agreed. She hadn't wanted her family to know she was seeing someone tonight. They'd probably make a big deal out of it if they knew.

While she was getting ready for her non-date, Susan came in. 'Wow! You look nice. That's a gorgeous jumper. Where are you going?'

'I thought I'd go for a ride — maybe grab some coffee.'

'By yourself?' The way Susan cocked her eyebrow showed she didn't believe her.

'Yup,' she lied, avoiding her sister's curious eyes.

'There's coffee in the kitchen.'

Tracy knew Susan could always tell when she was lying or hiding something. She'd hoped she'd got better at fooling her sister over the years, but she very much doubted it. The one thing she'd never acquired had been a poker face, which was ironic considering she was a lawyer.

Susan stood there watching her as she finished dressing. Tracy risked a look at her and knew from the skeptical look on her sister's face that she wasn't going to get anything past her. Susan wasn't going to let her go until she admitted the truth. She briefly contemplated using her sister's secrecy concerning Carrie's father as justification for her own, but it wasn't worth risking putting her sister on the defensive — although Tracy had every intention of getting the truth from Susan before she returned to London. If Carrie's father didn't want to help raise her that was fine; Carrie had plenty of people to love her, but Susan shouldn't have to support the child alone.

Tracy turned to face her sister. Time was running out, and if she didn't get going, she'd be late. Susan stood there staring at her, her arms crossed, looking a lot like a younger version of their mother.

Tracy had to laugh. 'Carrie won't stand a chance; you've got Mum's glare down to a tee.'

That got her attention. 'What do you mean by that? I'm nothing like Mum.'

'Said the pot to the kettle!' Tracy mimicked the pose her sister was doing.

Susan dropped the pose and replaced it with a pointed look. 'Are you going to tell me where you're really going or not?'

Tracy felt guilty for teasing her. She had a feeling there was more to her sister's curiosity than she was letting on, but she didn't have time to explore that right now. She hadn't spent much quality time with Susan since she'd arrived, other than the brief conversation they'd had last night, and most of that had been about Mike. She relented.

'I'm going to meet Mike O'Neill for coffee, okay?'

'What?' Her sister actually squealed and bounced up and down. 'You're going on a date with Mike O'Neill? Oh my God!' Susan had reverted to a teenager in an instant.

'It's not a date. It's just coffee.' Even to her own ears, her statement sounded false.

'Oh, it's a date,' Susan insisted. 'How did you manage that? He doesn't go out with any of the women around here, and believe me, many have tried!'

'I didn't do anything special. I asked, and he said yes.' She stepped around her sister, who was blocking the bedroom door. 'I have to go or else I'll be late.'

'Fine, but I want details when you get home.' The look on Susan's face promised a grilling the likes of which

Tracy hadn't had in ages.

'It's not a date!'

'Whatever you say,' Susan chuckled. As Tracy headed down the stairs, her sister called out, 'Have fun!'

★　★　★

Mike stood in the bathroom, tidying up the mess he'd made earlier when the phone had rung. He'd jumped out of the shower, soaking wet, tripped over his discarded jeans, and thrown himself across the bed in an attempt to answer the call before it went to voicemail.

'Hello?' he'd huffed out, not taking the time to check to see who it was calling.

The sound of Tracy's voice had made his ordeal to answer the phone worth it.

'Hi! It's me. How are you?' He'd heard the uneasiness in her voice. She'd seemed so self-assured earlier in the day, but the woman was a mystery. As confident as she seemed one minute, there were other times when he'd glimpsed the shy girl from the past.

'I'm fine, thanks. Are we still on for coffee?' He hoped she wasn't going to bail on him.

'Absolutely; I love my caffeine. Where do you want to meet? I could come and pick you up. I have an extra helmet.'

'No, that's okay. We can meet in front of the shop in about an hour, if that works for you?'

'I can manage that. See you then.' She'd hung up before he could say goodbye.

He'd pressed the end call button and returned to the bathroom. Now, standing in his bedroom, dressed in nothing but a towel, he wondered if just meeting for a coffee was enough.

He considered the matter for a few moments, and then decided it wasn't. A ride out into the countryside would be a much better idea. It was a beautiful, crisp, clear night, and she had no idea he owned a bike. He knew exactly where he'd take her.

He headed into the bathroom to

finish getting ready when his phone rang again. For a brief moment he debated letting it ring, in case it might be Tracy calling to cancel. If he didn't answer, he didn't think she'd stand him up.

He looked at the call display and saw it was his mother. He couldn't ignore her call.

'Hi, Mum. Is everything okay?'

'Hi, love. Yes, everything's fine. Jack and Lesley said to tell you hello and Merry Christmas. Of course, your sister would have loved to come home, but it's only fair that they spend Christmas with Jack's family this year. And the kids are happy with the presents we brought over for them. They love the idea of having two Christmases!'

'They'll be home next year,' he said, knowing how much his mum missed her daughter and grandchildren.

'Well, anyway, enough about all that. What have you been up to? Any plans for tonight?'

'As a matter of fact, yes. I'm going for

a moonlight ride.'

'Alone?' Suspicion laced her voice.

'No. I'm going with Tracy Stewart.'

'Really?' His mother's voice went up at least two octaves. He could hear the wheels turning in her head and sense her excitement. Belatedly, he remembered that his parents and the Stewarts were friends. Great! He should have kept his mouth shut.

'Don't read anything in to it, Mum. It's just a bike ride,' he cautioned. 'She even has her own bike.' But he knew it probably wouldn't stop her from thinking and planning.

'Fine. Have it your way, but you're not getting any younger, you know. It's time you settled down. Any woman would be lucky to have you.'

'So you keep saying. Although, as Tracy's just home for Christmas, I think a marriage proposal at this time would be a little premature.' He was surprised to realise, as he said it, that the idea of marriage to Tracy didn't scare him half to death. He could think of worse ways to spend his nights.

'Ha! Ha! Very funny.' He was glad he'd made her laugh, but doubted she'd let go of any matchmaking notions she might have.

'Mum, I have to go; I'm running late.'

'Wait! You'll pick us up at the airport tomorrow, yes?'

'Yes, I'll be there. Bye, Mum.'

'In a minute! You're always in a rush. Did you speak to Mrs. Harper?'

'Yes, I saw her earlier today. I assured her I'd be there first thing tomorrow morning to make a start setting up the stalls.'

'Thank you. I knew we could count on your help.' The pride in her voice was evident.

Mike enjoyed living in Eyam and being part of the close-knit community there. He'd spent four years in Edinburgh and then, after graduating, he'd worked for three years in London as an editor in a big publishing house. For a little while he'd been happy, but then the loneliness had crept up on him. Instead of reaching out and becoming more social, he'd retreated into himself as he'd done in his teenage years. When his father had announced his plans to sell the shop, Mike had left his job and come home. He'd never regretted his decision.

'Mum, I really do have to go now. I'll see you tomorrow. Have a safe flight.'

'Love you,' she said.

'Love you too. Give everyone a kiss for me.' He ended the call.

He needed to hurry. The last thing he wanted to do was make Tracy wait for him and worry he might not show up. He hoped she'd like his new plan for tonight.

4

Mike paced the pavement in front of the shop. He'd checked his watch twice in the last three minutes. What if his plan was a mistake?

He needed to get a grip! It was just a date, for heaven's sake. So what if it was the first date he'd had in Eyam? It wasn't like he'd been a monk or anything. He just didn't like playing in his own back garden. He liked his life simple, without drama. It was better that way. Guarding his privacy had become a survival mechanism. When he'd returned to Eyam and started fulfilling his lifelong passion for writing, he'd had no idea his first book would become such a success, let alone lead to others. He'd been awed and a little terrified by the sudden notoriety. To have people compare him to other great writers was a little overwhelming. He wrote mysteries; he was no William Shakespeare.

The writing had resulted in a financial security he'd only dreamed of enjoying. He was set for life. He could do whatever he wanted — the only problem was, he didn't know what he wanted. He did know that, whatever it was, it would involve making Eyam home — and because he suspected Tracy couldn't, a future with her was out of the question, no matter how great he thought she might be.

Tonight was all about spending a few hours together getting to know one another. She was only going to be here for a couple of weeks, so why not make the most of the time they had? When he thought about it, she was the first girl he'd met in a long time who liked to ride — lots enjoyed being passengers, but it really wasn't the same thing.

He'd decided to take her to one of his favourite spots, Stanage Edge, about half an hour's ride from Eyam. He loved night rides and walks along the edge, and he'd discovered this particular spot years ago when he'd first come back to Eyam.

At night, as in the daytime, the Peaks were alluring, but the area was also filled with jutting rocks and quick drops. You quickly learned to keep to the path. At night it was harder to tell the difference between what was safe and what was definitely a no-no, but that was part of the attraction. Anyone who rode was a risk-taker. Living on the edge was part of it.

He'd brought a flask of coffee and a picnic rug, and planned to sit on the large rock that looked down to Burbage Edge. As dangerous as the rocks could be, they had a stark beauty that couldn't be matched. He'd also added a strong LED torch in his box and had decided to give her a reading from G.L.'s latest book.

He'd walked through the bookshop earlier in the day looking for the right thing to impress her on their first date.

Tracy didn't seem like a flowers-and-chocolates kind of girl, but he knew she loved books. He'd picked up some poetry and a couple of classics, but from what she'd said, he hoped she'd enjoy a reading of his book. He'd just have to keep his fingers crossed she hadn't had time to start the book since she'd bought it.

You're putting a lot of effort into trying to impress a girl who's leaving the village in a couple of weeks, he thought to himself, but before he could analyse it any further he heard the sound of Tracy's bike approaching. He looked down the street to see her hunched over the bike, almost as if she and the machine were one, and he felt a jolt of desire run through him. Taking Tracy out into the Peaks in the moonlight might not be the wisest thing to do, but it was definitely what he wanted to do.

She pulled up alongside his bike, turned off her engine, and lifted the visor on her helmet. Her beautiful, large hazel eyes twinkled with excitement and curiosity.

'Nice ride! Is it yours?' She indicated the bike.

He walked over to where she sat astride her bike, his helmet dangling from his hand. The warm sensation he'd felt watching her approach pooled in his gut.

'Yes, she's mine; I thought we'd go for a ride over to Stanage Edge. The Peaks are just as beautiful a place at night as in the day, and I'd like to show you one of my favourite spots.'

'I don't know,' she said playfully. 'I was really looking forward to that cup of coffee.'

'Already taken care of — I've packed a flask full of my favourite blend. I took your word for it when you said you loved your caffeine. This stuff should do the trick.'

She laughed. He loved the sound of her laughter, and hoped he'd hear more of it before the night was over.

'Which way do we ride?'

'South on the B6001.'

'Let's go then.' She pushed down her visor, started the engine, and rode off.

He shook his head ruefully. He was going to have a really hard time keeping up with this woman, and not just because of her bike. He had a feeling the time spent with her was going to be one hell of a ride. He jumped on his bike and took off after Tracy, eager for the challenge.

They took turns taking the lead as they raced along the country road. He was really enjoying himself, far more than he had in a long time. As they sped along, the light from the moon turned the road into a silver ribbon stretching endlessly ahead of them. He could go on this way forever, but knowing that they'd have time to enjoy the eerie beauty of the star-studded Derbyshire sky and the miles of wild Peaks awash in the moonlight made him anxious to reach their destination. He'd contemplated using it as the setting in his next book. All depending on how things went tonight, he might.

He took the lead and turned onto a side road anyone might miss unless they knew it was there. He slowed his bike to make sure Tracy was behind him and to accommodate the change in road conditions. The hard-packed dirt road was better suited to off-road vehicles; it wasn't meant for street bikes, so some level of caution was necessary.

Maybe this wasn't such a good idea. What if Tracy got hurt? She probably wasn't used to this kind of terrain, and her ride looked brand new.

She pulled up beside him, signalled for him to hurry up a bit, and took the lead with confidence and dexterity. That might be a new bike, but he realised she wasn't a green rider. She could take care of herself.

When they reached the end of the road they shut off their bikes and made sure they were secure on the uneven ground. He took the backpack full of supplies out of his box and fastened his helmet and riding gloves to the bike as she was doing. He loved it here, and he hoped that after tonight she would too. If she did, she might come back to Eyam again, if only for the ride. He flipped the switch on the LED torch.

He held out his hand to her, and she took it without hesitation. Her hand was so small compared to his, and he stood almost a foot taller than her. He wasn't normally attracted to delicate women because he saw himself as a clumsy oaf next to them. They were so small, so fragile, and so breakable. The size difference between them had been there all along, but not once since he'd first laid eyes on her had he ever thought of her as dainty, and the way she rode her bike proved it.

'Where are we going?' She smiled when he looked at her. Her smile was almost as beautiful as her laugh.

'You'll see.' He shouldered the backpack he'd stuffed with the items they'd need. He made a point of damping down the excessive excitement

68

he felt running through him as they walked towards their destination.

★ ★ ★

Tracy had enjoyed the ride with Mike and was anxious to see where he was taking her. She'd been busy securing her gear and hadn't noticed what he'd put in the rucksack, but she was positive it was more than just a flask of coffee and two cups. The feel of his hand cradling hers was stirring sensations inside her that she wasn't ready to explore.

She told herself not to overthink it, to savour the moment — to enjoy the ride. She was only going to be back for a short time and if a gorgeous man wanted to spend time with her, then why not?

After years of living in London, where the city lights all but obliterated the stars, the night sky in Eyam resembled black velvet shot through with diamonds. The moon silvered the various shapes rising through the trees. It was both eerie and strangely romantic, but she wouldn't want to stray too far away from the path, and Mike.

She could see why he loved this place. It had an unearthly, haunting beauty that called to the soul. The Peaks rose up out of the blackness. How could she have lived here for eighteen years and not been out here?

Mike flashed the torch across the surface of the ground. 'Around about here looks like a good spot. A bit sheltered from that wind.' He pulled a picnic rug out of the rucksack and spread it on the ground. He continued pulling objects out of his bag, his back to her. He pulled out a lantern and turned it on, the white light creating an island of radiance amid the darkness. He turned off the torch to save the batteries.

It was colder in the Peaks than it had been in village, and Tracy was amused and relieved to see Mike pull out a thermos and a very cosy-looking blanket. While Mike was busy setting up, Tracy released her hair from the ponytail she'd worn under her helmet and watched as he poured coffee into heavy plastic mugs.

'How d'you take your coffee?' he asked, turning around to face her.

The friendly smile on his face died, replaced by a stunned look that almost made her laugh. Her hair was tousled and cascaded to her shoulders. She smiled mischievously. 'Milk and sugar, please.'

The look he gave her unsettled her. His eyes started at the tip of her knee-high leather boots and travelled up. When he reached her eyes, desire was evident in his.

'You take my breath away,' he whispered. The intense heat in his eyes had her hesitating to take his hand when he held it out to her. He noticed her hesitation, and she could tell he was about to drop the hand, so she reached for it and allowed him to guide her to the blanket.

She was a grown woman; what was she so afraid of?

'This is a great place. Thanks for bringing me here.' She swallowed the emotions and sexual tension that were threatening to choke her. How had a cup of coffee turned into a romantic idyll in the moonlight?

She smiled at him. Right now, all she wanted to do was lean across the short distance and kiss his beautiful mouth. He arranged the blankets around her and then turned to prepare the coffee. He handed her a mug and nestled in beside her. An owl hooted in the distance, and she jumped.

'Don't worry; sound carries in the Peaks. That owl was at least a mile away, probably on the hunt for a mouse or another tasty morsel.'

'You know a lot about the Peaks, don't you?'

He nodded and sipped his coffee. They sat there, deep in their own thoughts, looking out into the darkness.

She was comfortable with him. Not many people understood that sitting in silence didn't mean something was wrong.

'Do you come out here a lot?' she asked and looked over at him. He was sitting, leaning against his backpack. He looked content and relaxed.

'This is one of my favourite places; I come out here whenever I need to clear my head, you know — get away from it all. When I'm here, I can think straight.'

'Do you often bring girls here?'

'No; actually, I've never brought anyone up here.' His reply stunned her.

'Never?' She found that hard to believe. 'Why not?'

'I've never met anyone I wanted to share this place with before. I thought you'd appreciate it — kindred spirits, I suppose.'

Suddenly the sky was ablaze with streaks of white light as several meteors tore across it in a natural fireworks display that left her breathless.

'Did you know that was going to

happen? If you did, I'm impressed. Moonlight and fireworks — what a way to set the mood!'

'Did I know there'd be a meteor shower tonight? Not really, but they're quite common around here at this time of year. You don't notice them so much in the village because of the street lights.' Putting down his empty mug, he stretched his body along the rug.

She cleared her throat. 'Well, it's incredible. I can't imagine a girl not being impressed with such a setting.'

His warm laughter washed over her. He reached for her and pulled her down so that she rested against him, both of them watching the display in the night sky above.

'Good thing I'd finished my coffee,' she scolded. She breathed in his scent, a mixture of the spicy aftershave she'd noticed in the shop, and the outdoors.

She'd never found anything to like about Eyam, but she liked being here with him. Despite what she'd said to Susan, this was definitely a date, an unusual and far more intimate one than she'd ever had. She'd been wined and dined, but something as simple and beautiful as this? Never! This night would become a memory she'd cherish. For a moment, she imagined what it might have been like if they'd ever spoken to one another in school. Might they have become friends? Boyfriend and girlfriend, even?

Nestling her head more deeply into his chest, she shared her thoughts. 'How come we weren't friends when I lived here?' The rise and fall of his chest was comforting, as was the deep, even beat of his heart.

'I didn't have the nerve to talk to girls back then. I was rather shy. Not to mention you were two years younger than I was. Can you imagine what cradle-snatching would have done to what little reputation I might have had?'

'Seriously, I think we could have been friends; it might have made life a little easier for both of us.'

He was twirling a strand of her hair

around his finger, and she liked the intimacy of it.

'We did talk once.'

'Did we? I don't remember that. When?'

'It was during my last year. There was a fete in the village and I'd watched you trying for over an hour to win a pink teddy bear holding a book. You almost managed it, but then I heard you tell your friend that you'd run out of money. When you walked away, I decided I was going to win that bear for you. It cost me close to ten quid, but I knew how much you wanted it.'

'I remember that now!' she exclaimed. 'How could I have forgotten?' It seemed, along with the bad memories of Eyam, she'd pushed away a lot of good ones too. She sat up to get a better look at his face, and was disappointed when she saw he had his eyes closed. He continued to speak.

'I looked everywhere for you once I'd won it. I thought you'd left. When I finally found you I said, very eloquently, 'Here you go.' You thanked me, and I walked away before you could say anything else.'

'Do you know, I think that was one of the happiest moments of my life back then — maybe ever. That bear sat on my bed every day until I left for university. I still have it; I can't believe I'd forgotten that.'

She moved over him, and he opened his eyes. She moved her face closer to his and whispered against his lips, 'Thank you, Mike.' She kissed him gently, barely touching him.

5

The soft brush of her lips surprised him, but like food offered to a starving man, he wasn't going to refuse it. Mike groaned deep in his throat. He entwined his fingers in her silky hair and pulled her closer, pressing her body into his.

When she didn't pull away, he deepened the kiss, giving free rein to the urgency within him. She let her eyes close, and he shut his to block out everything but the sensation of her lips on his. Her mouth was made for kissing — lush full lips, pulsing and throbbing with life beneath his, lips he'd dreamed of kissing from the second she'd sauntered into his shop.

His libido screamed for more, but his common sense warned him that if he didn't stop now there would be no turning back. This wasn't what he'd been expecting, and he wasn't prepared for it.

'I know I'm going to regret this, and it may very well kill me to do so, but we need to stop.' Contrary to what his words said, he continued to feather her face with gentle kisses. Every time his lips moved away from her, he could feel the air stealing away the taste and texture of her, and he didn't like it.

Tracy smiled against his lips. 'If you want me to try and control myself, you'll have to stop kissing me like this,' she murmured, running her fingers lightly through his hair, exciting him further, and sending a surge of desire through his body.

'Believe me, I am trying, but I just can't seem to get enough of you. You're addictive.'

She leaned down, pressing her chest to his, bringing her delicate hands up slowly to caress his face. He could feel her warm breath on his lips as she ran her fingers through his hair again. He ached for her.

With what little willpower he had left, he lifted her from him, cradling her so he wouldn't hurt her, and gently flipped her onto her back, straddling her so that she bore none of his body weight, but pinning her to the rock beneath them. His eyes met hers, surprised by the level of heat and desire he saw there. Both of them panted, hearts beating at an incredible rate, their lungs barely able to filter enough oxygen out of the air, as they tried to calm their overheated bodies.

He kissed her one last time — a long, drugging kiss that promised more. He slowly lifted himself off her and reached for the rucksack. He removed the book he'd brought. He turned back toward her and stopped, awed by what he saw.

Her tangled hair was spread across the blanket; her lips were ruby-red and swollen from his kisses; her eyes were sparkling, dark amber gems in the light of the lantern. She was the most alluring woman in the world, and at the moment she was all his. Using his backpack as a pillow he lay down, pulling her into and slightly onto him, so she could rest her head against his shoulder. Her breathing was still ragged, and he knew it wouldn't take much to send them both tumbling into oblivion again. He wasn't sure he'd be able to stop the next time.

'I brought a book, and I thought I'd read to you.' He tried to ignore the softness of her body moulded to his.

'You're going to read to me?' Her voice was shaky and surprised.

'I thought you'd like that. Was I wrong?'

She shook her head. 'No. I love being read to. What did you bring?' She snuggled into him; he felt her shiver. He pulled an unused portion of the blanket over her.

'G.L. O'Michael's latest book. You haven't started it yet, have you?'

'Good choice,' she chuckled. 'I haven't had much time for reading anything but children's books since I've been back.'

He opened the book and stroked her hair as he read, stopping only to turn the pages. Before he'd finished chapter two, he heard her soft snores. So much for his engrossing prose!

He closed the book softly. He stretched his arm behind his head, making himself comfortable, and listened to Tracy's soft breathing. He'd never felt so contented.

He ran his fingers through her soft, wavy hair. If this wasn't a perfect moment, it was certainly close. He closed his eyes and matched her, breath for breath.

★   ★   ★

It was almost midnight when they returned to the village and pulled up in front of his place. He'd offered to escort her to her mother's, but she'd declined.

She stood by her bike and he moved to gather her into his arms, hoping he could convince her to come inside for a bit, but instead she looked at the house and said disbelievingly, 'You still live at your parents' house?'

'They aren't around much, so it doesn't make sense for me to have a place of my own when this one's empty most of the time.' Her tone of voice had surprised him.

'Right. Okay. Well, I'd better get going. Thanks for a wonderful evening. Sorry for falling asleep on you. Don't mention it to G.L. It really wasn't the story — I just haven't been getting much sleep lately. I've been burning the candle at both ends at work so I could get this time off.'

'Wouldn't you like to come in for a real drink?' He couldn't believe she was planning to leave it at this.

'No. I make it a point not to drink and ride. I promised Mum no one would ever have to scrape me off the road, plus I've got so much to do tomorrow, and as you saw, I clearly need to get some rest.' She gave him a quick kiss and mounted her bike. 'I'll call you.' She put on her helmet, dropped the visor in place, and started the bike.

*　*　*

Tracy pulled away from the kerb without looking back, intent on getting home as quickly as she could. Tonight had been wonderful; in fact, it had been perfect — until he'd invited her into his parents' house.

Really? His parents' house? What was a man his age doing still living with his mum and dad? The bookshop couldn't possibly be doing that badly.

She could almost understand his reasoning. Since they weren't there much, it made sense, but still. She couldn't imagine it. She wanted — needed — her own space, her own things, her own life, for goodness' sake.

Of course Susan lived at home, but that was different. She was a single mother with a two-year-old to look after, as well as her own business to manage. She needed help, but Mike was a grown man. He should want to have his own place. She couldn't understand why in the world he'd give up life in London to come back to Eyam and live with his parents. It made no sense.

She pulled into the driveway and parked the bike beside the house, ignoring the voice in her head that kept telling her she was overreacting. She eased the door open, hoping everyone was asleep so she wouldn't have to play twenty questions as to where she'd been and why she was so late coming in. Relief washed over her when she reached her room unheard.

She opened the door quickly, confident that she'd soon be in bed, and smothered a scream when she saw someone sitting in the old rocker by the window.

'Susan! You scared me half to death! What are you doing here? It's after midnight.'

'Shush! You don't want to wake Mum or Carrie,' her sister whispered. 'I told you, I wanted details. So . . . ?'

'I don't believe this; you camped out in my room, waiting for me to come home?'

'Yes.'

'You're mad!' She plopped down onto her bed. All she wanted to do was sleep and forget the totally gorgeous guy who had just taken her on the date of a lifetime — and who still lived with his mum.

'No, Tracy, just lonely.' The sadness in Susan's voice made Tracy open her eyes and look properly at her sister. The look of longing on her face broke Tracy's heart. 'Humour me, please,' Susan begged.

'Fine. Come on.' She motioned to the bed beside her. The irony of the role reversal didn't escape her. In years past, it had been Tracy who'd sat anxiously waiting to hear all about her sister's escapades.

Tracy saw excitement animate her sister's face as she scrambled to get comfortable. She grabbed an extra pillow, placed it on Tracy's chest and rested her head on it.

'Tell me everything — don't leave out a single detail,' she commanded as Tracy unconsciously began to twirl a strand of her sister's hair around her finger the way she'd done years ago — the way Mike had done with hers tonight.

'Okay.' Tracy's smile was bittersweet. She realised how much she'd missed the nights spent like this with her sister.

'We didn't exactly go for coffee,' she began.

Susan sat up so quickly Tracy cried out in surprise. 'Watch it! You almost hit me.'

'Sorry.' Susan smiled and shrugged her shoulders. 'I want to see your face while you talk. Go on.'

'Did you know Mike had a motorcycle?' she asked.

'Yes. I've seen him riding it a few times. He's a real man of mystery. He keeps to himself, and I think that adds to his appeal.'

'Absolutely!' Tracy saw the interest on Susan's face. She wasn't sure how she felt about Mike, but she did know the idea of him with another woman, especially her sister, bothered her. 'Are you interested in him?'

Susan laughed.

'I wish I were.' Her response piqued Tracy's interest.

'What does that mean?'

'Nothing. Mike's a good guy. I have a tendency to go after bad boys.'

'Would you call Carrie's father a bad boy?'

Susan looked at her impatiently. 'We've been over this time and time again. Carrie's father is not up for discussion.'

'Susan, you can't make a comment like that and not give me something. Was he abusive? Did he hurt you?'

'Oh no, nothing like that. I just should have known better. So, if you didn't go for coffee, where did Mike take you?'

Knowing she wouldn't get any more

out of Susan tonight, Tracy described her amazing night with Mike, omitting nothing about the earth-shattering kisses they'd shared.

'So he invited you in for a drink, and you said no?' Susan's confusion was evident in the tone and the look on her face.

'Yes.'

'Why on earth would you say no? What you've described sounds like the most romantic night I can imagine. You've just said you could barely control yourself when he was kissing you.'

'I don't know. I'm tired, Susan. I need sleep.'

She could tell from Susan's face that her sister knew she wasn't being up-front about everything, but she didn't want to talk about it any more. She wasn't sure she understood it herself. Susan confirmed her suspicions when she said, 'Rubbish.'

'Go to bed, Sue.'

'Tracy?'

'Look. You have your secrets, I have mine,' Tracy said — and immediately regretted it. She could be such an idiot!

Susan bristled. 'Good night.' Without another word, she let herself out of the room and closed the door behind her.

'Damn!'

Tracy got undressed and into bed, but sleep eluded her. She punched her pillow repeatedly, tossing and turning, trying to get comfortable. She wanted to forget the way her body had reacted to Mike. She wanted to wipe the memory of his kiss from her mind, but she couldn't. And why did his living arrangements bother her so much?

She heard the sound of her phone vibrating against the surface of the bedside table and glanced at the clock. It was well after one. Who could be calling at this hour? She checked the call display — Mike.

She stared at the phone. Should she answer it or just let him go?

6

Tracy swiped at the sweat beading on her forehead and sighed. She loved her sister and was incredibly proud of her success, but she was beginning to regret volunteering to help her out today. Sweet Buns, Susan's coffee shop and bakery, was her dream come true. Susan loved the shop's name, Mum thought it was scandalous — once the play on the word 'buns' had been explained to her — and Tracy believed it was just the right side of cheeky, and perfect for the small business her sister had grown into such a thriving enterprise.

The High Street had been busy all morning with people coming and going, some to help and others just to look at the preparations on the go for tomorrow's Christmas Fair. It seemed as if everyone in the village had stopped by to sample some of Susan's wares or pick up bread or rolls for dinner. Her sticky buns were a particular favourite, and after sampling one earlier Tracy could understand why. No wonder her sister's business was doing so well.

Tracy had arrived at the bakery at eight, three hours after Susan, who'd come in at her usual five in the morning to do the early-morning baking. She'd been wary at the thought of seeing the people of Eyam. Since she'd returned home she'd done a good job of avoiding them — well, maybe not all of them, but those she felt had snubbed her all those years ago.

She recognised many of the customers, and those who recognised her were full of questions about her life in London and praise for how successful she'd become. It was strange; she couldn't remember anyone ever asking about her before. Now, she seemed to be some kind of celebrity. A twinge of guilt ate at her more than once when she realised people genuinely cared about her and were happy to see her. She couldn't recall ever asking about anything or anyone in Eyam, and she regretted it. She wished she could stop and chat longer with each person, but the place was so busy she had to rush just to keep up. It had been a long time since her waitressing years and her feet, back and legs were loudly protesting this new torture she'd discovered for them.

Seeing her old English teacher, Mr. Beveton, the man she'd been certain had been put on earth for the sole purpose of making her life as miserable as possible, had been a shock. While he'd aged, it had been his attitude towards her that had amazed her. He'd been happy and excited to see her, telling her how proud he was of her accomplishments, and even confessing that she'd been one of his favourite students. Others, people she'd thought barely aware of her existence back then, had commented on how lovely it was to see her again, and she was certain she'd never blushed and laughed so much in her life. Even Mrs. Harper, the village busybody, had said nice things to her. It had felt good to feel as if she belonged, even if it was for a short time.

Despite the thrill of discovering that the people of Eyam didn't resemble those in her memory, she cringed each time the door opened and the bell rang announcing a new customer. There was someone she wasn't ready to see right now. She hadn't answered the phone last night, but her sleep had been plagued by dreams that had her waking up frustrated and just as confused as when she went to bed.

Why hadn't she answered the phone? Did she want to see Mike again? She kept trying to convince herself that she didn't, but the thought of never feeling his arms around her again dismayed her. She tried to convince herself that she didn't need a man like him in her life — a man who made her feel alive and more aware of herself as a woman than anyone ever had, a man who got under her skin and wouldn't be easy to leave behind when she returned to London. That was the problem. She wanted him, but she didn't want Eyam, and she had a feeling they were inseparable — and then there was the whole living at home thing that confused her. Each time the bell sounded, she practically got whiplash making sure the customer wasn't him — so why was she so disappointed each time it wasn't?

Thank goodness Sweet Buns was so busy that she couldn't dwell for too long on thoughts of Mike, but that didn't seem to stop her mind from dragging him to the forefront. She'd caught a glimpse of the volunteers putting up wreaths and erecting stalls, and she thought she'd seen him, but it must have been her overactive imagination.

By the middle of the afternoon business had slowed enough that they were able to sit down with a muffin and a mug of coffee and rest their aching feet. With the shop quiet for the moment they were able to talk — a rare luxury, apparently, on Saturdays. Tracy savoured every bite of her chocolate muffin and sipped the rich dark coffee, similar in flavour to what Mike had produced last night.

After her sleepless night, she was exhausted. She couldn't imagine how Susan did this day after day. She'd only been here a few hours, whereas Susan worked twelve-hour days, six days a week, and then went home to care for a toddler. She'd been proud of her sister before, but today her admiration grew exponentially.

'We did well today.' Susan reached for her coffee and sipped. 'It's probably the busiest Saturday I've had since Halloween, and I think the fact that you're here brought in a few customers I haven't seen before. I hope they'll come back now that they've sampled my wares. Maybe I should consider having a celebrity work here once a month.'

Tracy laughed. 'But where will you find a celebrity in Eyam once I'm gone? Anyway, if this muffin and the sticky bun I ate earlier today are any indication, they'd be fools not to come back. By the way, this coffee is delicious, better than anything I can get in London. What's your secret?'

'I buy the best Arabica beans I can find. I keep them in a sealed glass jar and grind them as I go. I only make small pots and never keep brewed coffee more than an hour. It's all about freshness.' She laughed. 'Before I started this place, I made the world's worst cup of coffee. Tasted like dishwater!'

Tracy enjoyed the animation on her sister's face. Susan clearly loved the shop, regardless of the long hours that went with it. Tracy watched as Louise, the part-time baker, refilled the display counter once more with what was left of the day's cakes. Susan made all of the raw products first thing in the morning, and Louise saw that everything was baked and displayed as needed. Bread had to rise, so it was prepared late the previous afternoon, and as it was ready, she put the loaves in or took them out of the industrial ovens in the kitchen.

Since it was Saturday, Susan would come in tomorrow for a while to set the bread and make up all the extra batches of shortbread biscuits that had been ordered for Christmas. She decorated all of the regular cakes and cupcakes herself, as well as any specialty cakes that had been pre-ordered. Tracy had watched in awe earlier this morning when Susan decorated a cake that looked like a kilt with a set of bagpipes beside it.

'Fergus will be one hundred years old on Monday, and his daughter ordered this birthday cake for the celebration. It's taken days to complete,' said Susan. 'The plaid kilt was the hardest.'

'It's amazing.' She stared at her sister's creation. 'I had no idea how creative and talented you were.'

The front door opened. Tracy groaned inwardly as Susan hopped off the chair, flashing her welcoming smile. *Here we go again.* She dreaded the possibility she might needed to stand.

'Hello, Mr. White.' Susan's voice was full of enthusiasm, as if seeing this customer was the high point of her day.

'Hello, Susan. Merry Christmas. How are you?'

'We're doing well. You look better; has that cough finally gone?' Tracy watched her sister make small talk and realised she'd done so with each of her customers. How did she manage to keep track of the minutiae of their daily lives?

'Yes, finally. I'll bet that little angel of yours is eager for Christmas.'

'She certainly is. Santa had better come soon. Her list keeps growing. Where's Mrs. White?'

'She's just picking up some last-minute things. She should be along any minute. Can I have a coffee and a couple of your chocolate brownies?'

'You certainly can.' Susan turned to fill his order.

'I'll go over and sit with Tracy.'

His words surprised Tracy, but she sat up straighter and smiled as he walked toward her.

'Hello Tracy. I'm glad to see you. I was hoping I'd have a chance to talk to you while you were here. May I?' He indicated the seat Susan had vacated. Tracy nodded.

'Hi, Mr. White. It's nice to see you too. You wanted to talk to me? About what?' She couldn't imagine what the man could possibly want with her. Susan brought over his coffee and brownies and went back to the counter.

The door opened and Mrs. White hurried in with her hands so full of bags, it was a miracle she could carry them. She walked right over to the table where her husband sat and gave him a peck on the cheek. The simple sign of affection made Tracy smile. Mrs. White dropped into the third chair at the table and turned to Tracy.

'Merry Christmas! Tracy, you look marvellous. We just saw Edna; she told us you were in here,' she said, giving Tracy a pleasant smile. 'Just coffee for me, dear,' she called out to Susan. 'Have you asked her, John?' She touched her husband's arm to get his attention.

'Not yet. I just got here. I haven't even had time to taste my coffee yet.'

Tracy's curiosity was piqued. Mr. White, the village's resident lawyer for more than thirty years, wanted to ask her something and judging by his wife's comment it was important.

'I have a proposition for you, Tracy. Let me get straight to the point.' He used his best courtroom voice. 'When your mother told me you were coming home for Christmas, I decided to put off placing an advertisement in the paper until after I'd spoken to you. Give a local girl a go first.'

Tracy was confused. A local girl? She didn't consider herself a local girl. She hadn't even visited this place in ten years.

'I don't understand. A go at what?'

'My practice, of course. I've decided to retire and do some travelling. I've been promising to take the missus to Pompeii for the past thirty years. I thought it was time to make good on that promise.'

Tracy saw the happy glow on Mrs. White's face. A pang of envy struck her. What would it be like to have someone special in your life for that long? She thought of her mum and dad. Unexpectedly, a vision of Mike entered her mind. What would it be like to spend thirty years with him?

Susan brought Mrs. White's coffee over as Mr. White continued. 'I wanted to know if you would be interested in assuming my practice. I'm sure we could work out suitable terms. I wouldn't expect you to pay it all up front, and I'd still be around to help you out until you got comfortable with the work.'

Before she could fully grasp what he'd said, Susan squealed. 'Oh my goodness, Tracy! That would be wonderful. You could come home, and we could all be together again.'

Tracy was dismayed. She cursed inwardly. Why hadn't Mr. White waited until she was alone to broach the matter? Neither he nor Susan would be happy with the only answer she could give. She smiled to take the sting out of her words.

'Thank you, Mr. White; it's a wonderful offer, but I have to say no. I have a career in London, and I'll be going back after Christmas. I've no intention of staying in Eyam.' She avoided looking at her sister, knowing that she'd see pain and accusation there.

'Now, don't be hasty. Why don't you take a few days to think about it? I know I've sprung this on you rather suddenly, and while it would be a big change from working with a large established firm the way you do in London, it does have its advantages. I'll wait until after the New Year to post the ad. I'd really hate to have an outsider taking over the private legal concerns of my clients. I know the people of Eyam would be comfortable with you handling things.'

Tracy wanted to tell him not to waste his time, but she couldn't. There was no way she was going to move back here to stay — ever — but she knew arguing with Susan in front of Mr. White wouldn't be the smartest thing to do.

'All right, I'll see you before I leave the village,' she lied. She hated to stretch the truth, but at the moment she saw no other alternative. She'd given him her answer, and he'd refused to accept it — but she'd made her decision, and it wasn't going to change.

Mr. White smiled broadly. 'Good. I know when you think about it, you'll see the benefit of owning your own firm. Now, we have to get going.' He and Mrs. White stood.

'Can we have a loaf of that twelve-grain bread, please?' Mrs. White approached the counter.

'Of course.' Tracy could see her sister was forcing herself to be pleasant. She was angry and disappointed, but that was too bad. Susan had her life to live, and she had hers.

After the Whites left the shop, Susan came over to stand next to Tracy. She'd hoped to avoid this conversation until later — maybe even avoid it altogether, but the shop was empty, and there was nowhere to run.

'Aren't you even going to consider his offer?' Susan asked point-blank.

'No, I'm not. I gave him my answer. He didn't want to accept it, but it isn't going to change.' She saw the pain her words inflicted on her sister, but they were the truth. 'I have no intention of ever returning to live in Eyam.'

'Why not? Eyam is home. This would be a great opportunity for you. The business is established, and you wouldn't have to work such long hours. We could be a family again.'

'You're missing the point, Sue. I like the life I've made for myself in London. I'm proud of what I've accomplished, and I'm on the fast track to a big promotion. I can make partner one day. This shop is your dream, that partnership is mine. I don't want to give it up.'

'Aren't you lonely? Don't you miss us?' Susan's eyes filled with tears.

'Of course I miss you all; don't be ridiculous. But we're still family, no matter where I live.' She could see tears rolling slowly down her sister's cheeks. 'I've worked really hard to get where I am, just as you have. If I leave now, it'll all have been for nothing.'

'Don't say that! It wouldn't be for nothing.' Susan's anger replaced her pain. 'It would be for us — our family. I know what you went through — the long hours, the way you juggled university and waitressing, the sacrifices you've made. I don't know how you did it, especially so far from home and without any help. When you passed the bar and got the position in London, I thought things would get better, but they didn't. The hours got longer, and you had even less time for us than you'd had before. If you said yes to Mr. White, you'd be the owner of the firm, your own boss, and we'd be here for you, just as you'd be here for us.'

Sorrow filled her. 'Susan, I wish I could, but . . . I just can't.'

'I don't believe that,' she answered. 'You could — you just don't want to.' She was about to add something else when the door opened.

'How are my girls?' Her dad entered the shop and stopped cold when he looked at them.

'Fine,' they answered in unison, one defiant, the other emotional.

Her father looked from one to the other, a frown replacing the smile he'd worn on his way in the door.

'You girls are fighting about something, aren't you? You know I don't like that.'

'Blame Tracy,' Susan said self-righteously. 'Mr. White offered to sell her his practice, and she declined without even giving it any thought. She doesn't care about any of us.'

'Susan!' cried Tracy. 'That's not fair!'

★ ★ ★

What Mike wouldn't give for a pair of earplugs right about now. From the second he'd met his parents at the airport, his mother hadn't stopped grilling him about Tracy. For the first time in as long as he could remember, his parents agreed on something that concerned him, and it was really none of their business.

It had been one date, a couple of fantastic, earth-shattering kisses, and one dismal, disappointing ending, but already his mum was planning the wedding and commenting on how adorable their children would be. It was driving him mad.

He'd just finished warning his

mother not to start spreading any rumours, when Tracy tore by him on her bike, exceeding the speed limit, going way too fast for road conditions and traffic. What on earth was wrong with her?

Mike pulled over to the side of the road, faking a headache, and asked his dad to drive the rest of the way home. He hopped into the back seat, the dark look on his face warning his mother not to speak. Sometimes a history of migraines came in handy. He doubted his parents had recognised her in her leathers riding her bike, but he wasn't prepared to discuss it at the moment. He knew Tracy's headset was equipped with Bluetooth, so he knew she'd be able to answer his call — but he tried a dozen times, and she wasn't picking up.

Visions of her wrapped around a telephone pole, or worse, played through his mind. He kept telling himself she'd be fine, but the reckless speed at which she'd been travelling had his nerves on edge. She'd promised her mother not to end up splattered on the roads; she'd keep that promise — he hoped.

As quickly as he decently could, he unloaded the car and ushered his parents into the house. It took twenty minutes to get himself out of there, into his own leathers, and onto his bike. He made two more attempts to reach her before she finally answered. The relief he felt when he heard her voice couldn't be measured, but it came across as anger. He'd never been so worried.

'Tracy, why haven't you been answering your phone?'

'I didn't feel like talking.'

Her comment stung, but he could tell she was upset. Something must have happened.

'I saw you fly past me on the road. You were moving like the wind; you scared the living daylights out of me.'

'I had to ride. I had to get away from that place. I was suffocating.'

He knew the feeling and understood

what she said better than anyone. He'd felt like that time and again.

'Is everything okay?' He'd heard the pain in her voice.

'No.'

'Do you want to talk about it?'

'Not really.'

'I may be able to help; I've been there once or twice.'

'Actually, you're the only one who can help.' Her voice sounded small and defeated.

He pulled his bike over so he could concentrate on the conversation. It was late afternoon, and the feeble winter sun was setting. Clouds in the distance promised rain before too long. He got off the bike and started to pace. 'Tell me what's wrong.'

'I'm lost.' She sounded as if she was about to cry, and it tore at his heart.

He remembered what it had been like to come home after so much time had passed. It had been overwhelming. He wanted to help Tracy through this, be with her, but he doubted it was the right time for that. She needed to deal with this first.

'Tracy, I know how hard it can be to come home, wondering if you still belong — whether you should stay or go. Why don't you tell me what happened to make you feel so lost?' He felt like a doctor, but after the way she hadn't answered the phone and driving that bike fast enough to break her neck, he'd be whoever she wanted him to be as long as she kept talking. He needed to hear the sound of her voice.

'What are you talking about? I'm lost, as in I don't know where the hell I am!' Anger and frustration replaced the panic in her voice he'd mistaken for sadness. How stupid could he be?

He turned and hurried back to the bike he'd left to concentrate on the call. It was getting darker by the minute. 'Lost? Where?'

'If I knew where I was, I wouldn't be lost, would I?' She sounded more than a little annoyed with him. 'I got into an argument with Susan and had to get away, so I decided to go to our place and clear my head. The only problem is, after I left the bike I didn't quite know which way to go, and now I'm lost in the dark and cold, and I want to go home.'

If knowing she was alone in the middle of the deserted Peaks at night didn't have him seriously concerned, the fact that she'd called it 'our place' would have thrilled him.

'Tracy, don't walk any further. Do you have a light?'

'Yes, a small torch, but the batteries are weak.'

'Okay, keep the light on and flash it around you — but whatever you do, don't move. I'm on my way.'

'Mike, please hurry; I don't think the torch is going to last long. I'm so cold! I can't believe how stupid I've been.'

He could tell she was getting close to a full-blown panic. The last thing he needed was for her to freak out and run deeper into the Peaks. There were rocks sharp enough to give you a nasty cut, the ground was uneven, and in places it just vanished.

'You'll be fine. I'll be there as soon as I can.'

He didn't say goodbye. He started the bike and drove as fast as he could. He had to try and find her before her torch went out.

7

Mike's mind filled with images of a freezing Tracy, lost and alone in the darkened hills, and he had to keep reminding himself to slow down. Crashing his bike and getting killed wouldn't help. When the turn-off for the dirt road came into sight, it didn't lessen his fears. The closer he got, the harder he found it to breathe.

He couldn't stop horrible scenarios from taking shape in his fertile imagination. At times like these his creative writer's mind was a curse, not a blessing. What if he just couldn't find her?

'Stupid! Stupid! Stupid!' He slammed his palm against his handlebar. He should never have brought her here. This was really all his fault. To the uninitiated, the meandering paths and rocks could look alike. Even if she thought she'd found the right place, she could easily be mistaken.

He sped down the dirt road far too quickly for its condition, but speed was of the essence. He needed to try and find her while there was still a little battery life left in her torch; it was the best chance they had. He wouldn't be able to live with himself if anything happened to her.

When he finally reached the end of the road he parked his bike next to hers, grateful to see she had at least made it this far safely. With any luck she was somewhere nearby.

He dismounted and looked around him, but he couldn't see light anywhere. He pulled out his mobile phone, hoping that the erratic signal out here was working and she wasn't in a dead spot. He made call after call, but her phone kept going to voicemail; either she had no signal or the battery had died. The possibility that she was injured and couldn't answer played on the edge of his mind, but he refused to give it credence.

He prayed she'd listened, stayed where she was, and hadn't moved further into the unknown darkness. He took a powerful LED torch out of his rucksack and headed towards his favourite spot, hoping that was the direction she'd taken.

After a few more attempts to reach her by phone, he gave up and stopped moving. He was at Stanage Edge, and she wasn't here. He scanned the area with the light and called out her name as loudly as he could. He listened, got no answer, and moved away from the rock.

He proceeded as quickly as he could, using the powerful torch to search the ground ahead of him, and continued to call her name, stopping each time he did, listening for her answer. When he heard her faint reply his heart, which had been pounding its way out of his chest as it was, sped up, and he veered in that direction, walking as quickly as he could over the uneven ground. He kept speaking to her, talking of nothing, but using the sound of her voice to narrow down her location. When he saw her silhouette against the blackness of the night, he wanted to run to her and take her in his arms. Relief flooded him.

He moved the last few feet to her side and gathered her in his arms, grateful to feel her there. The floodgates of her tears opened and she cried, exhaustion and relief a powerful mix. He held her tightly, murmuring words of comfort, raining kisses into her hair. When his breathing had returned to normal and her crying jag had abated, he slowly eased her away from him.

'Are you okay?' he asked.

'Yes. No! I don't know! I feel so stupid.'

He held her tightly, giving her a minute to gather herself. The sooner he got her home the better.

'I'm so sorry you had to come out here and rescue me,' she said sheepishly. 'I'm not usually the damsel-in-distress type. It was silly of me to come out here alone.'

'It was more than just silly. I'm not going to sugar-coat it — coming out here by yourself on a winter's night, when you don't know the area at all, was reckless.' The fear he'd felt reasserted itself, and his voice was angry.

She pushed him away, and he could see her indignation.

'I said I was sorry; don't worry. If I'm ever in trouble again, I'll be sure not to bother you.' She turned to walk off in the direction he'd come. He grabbed her arms, stopping her and turning her to face him.

'Listen to me! When I think about what could have happened . . . ' He couldn't bring himself to finish. He swallowed the lump in his throat and let out a breath, trying to calm himself. 'I don't know what I would have done if I hadn't found you.' His voice hitched. He pulled her back into his arms. She didn't resist. They stood, bathed in the light from the torch at their feet, where he'd dropped it.

He looked into her eyes and placed his quivering hand along the side of her face, wiping at the salt tracks of her tears with the pad of his thumb, stroking his finger across her trembling lips.

'I want to be the person you call when you need help, Tracy; I want to be the one you turn to, always.'

She smiled unsteadily at him, and his heart quickened.

'I'm sorry; you're right. Thank you for coming out here and saving me.' She leaned forward and placed a soft kiss on his mouth. It wasn't like the hungry kisses they'd shared the night before; this tender kiss was full of promise.

Perhaps after this she'd open up to him and trust him with her secrets. His conscience nagged at him though. Was it fair to want her to trust him when he wasn't ready to trust her? Pushing the irritating thought away, he deepened the kiss, grateful that she was safe and in his arms once more. She returned his kiss with an eagerness that spoke of her need to feel alive after her scare.

He released her lips slowly. 'I don't know about you, but I'm freezing. Come on; let's get back home.'

'Good idea, and as soon as we do, I'm going to need more than a coffee to settle my frazzled nerves.' She moved out of his arms, reached down and picked up the torch, handed it to him, and wrapped her fingers tightly around his.

Without a word, he turned and started to retrace his steps back to their bikes. The surroundings were as beautiful as they had been last night; however, right now it was the last place he wanted to be. He turned right and headed along the well-worn path to their bikes. He held her hand firmly in his, wondering if he'd ever feel safe enough to let it go.

She was still shivering when they arrived at the motorcycles.

'Can you ride?' he asked as she untied her helmet from the saddle where she'd secured it.

'I think so, but I'm still looking forward to that drink.'

'We'll park the bikes at my place and grab a cab to the Queen's Head; that suit you?'

'Sounds like a plan.'

Knowing she was safe had robbed him of his sanity, and he took the opportunity to steal one more kiss before she donned her helmet. He doubted she'd let him get this intimate in a crowded pub.

He'd never wanted a woman this badly before, and it scared him. The encounter had left him as shaky as she was, and he fought hard not to let her see it. She wasn't the only one who needed a drink. He'd made his point about the danger she'd been in; now all he wanted was to make her feel safe again.

'Do you want to talk about why you came out here in the first place?'

'No, I don't. Let's go and get that drink.'

'You're sure you're okay to drive now?'

'Yes, I'll be fine.'

He watched Tracy settling on her bike and did the same. He realised that what he'd seen as a harmless flirtation might have greater consequences than he'd imagined. Not wanting to dwell on the matter, he started up his bike and followed her.

* * *

Tracy felt relieved when she turned her bike into Mike's driveway, glad she'd be able to leave it here overnight. She still had to face her family, a daunting prospect she didn't think she could handle right now.

The bitter exchange with Susan after her sister had blurted out Mr. White's offer to her father had wounded her, but it been her sister's final, sad words that had haunted her as she fled the bakery: 'Just because you don't want to be here with us doesn't mean I'm going to make it easy for you to leave us again.'

Susan's statement had echoed in her mind as she'd stupidly sought Mike's place of refuge. Why was it so hard for her family to understand she didn't want to live in Eyam?

Pulling off her helmet, she secured the bike and turned to ask Mike to call the taxi when a woman opened the door to the house and called his name.

'Michael! Where have you been? You left in such a hurry. I've been worried sick.'

His parents were home! If she'd known that, she'd have refused to come. She still had trouble under-standing his living arrangements — having your mother race down the stairs to ask questions and berate you as if you were still a child was one of the reasons she couldn't bear the thought of coming back to Eyam herself. He had no privacy, and obviously, even over thirty, he still had to answer to someone. She stared at

Mike, waiting for the frustration and impatience she'd have felt in the same circumstances to surface, but it never came. Instead, he smiled at his mum and gave her a hug.

'Sorry about that. Tracy called. She got lost in the Peaks and needed help.'

Mrs. O'Neill had focused all her attention on her wayward son and hadn't noticed her behind him.

'Oh my goodness! Tracy, are you okay?'

'Yes, thank you, Mrs. O'Neill. I'm fine.' She hoped she sounded more self-assured than she felt.

'Come inside and I'll get you something to drink.' She took Tracy's arm and led her toward the steps.

'That's okay,' Tracy protested. 'I don't want to be any trouble.'

'Nonsense! You come inside for a few minutes. I know Jacob will be happy to see you.'

Tracy turned to Mike for support, but all she got was a shrug. She was on her own. She was going to wring his neck. What she needed was a good stiff shot of something, not a cosy chat with Mum and Dad.

Unable to graciously decline without Mike's help, she agreed to go in for a few minutes. Mrs. O'Neill beamed at her acceptance and led her towards the house. Tracy was pretty sure Mike was smirking behind her. She didn't dare look back because if he were, she wouldn't be able to stop herself from punching him.

Once inside, she sat on the couch in the living room. It had been ten years since she'd seen Mr. O'Neill, but he hadn't changed much. Looking at the two men together, she realised how much Mike resembled his father. At their insistence, she recapped how she'd got herself lost and Mike had rescued her. Tracy could hear Brenda gasping while she was getting drinks in the kitchen. Within a matter of minutes, she returned to the living room with glasses and a bottle of brandy that she placed on the coffee table.

She poured a generous amount of the liquid in a glass and handed it to Tracy. 'I have wine or tea, but I think after your ordeal you'll appreciate this more.'

'You're right. Thanks.'

Tracy took a sip and leaned back on the couch. The emotional highs and lows of the day had taken their toll, and she was bone tired. Mike leaned back and put his arm around her shoulders, pulling her into his side. She saw the raised eyebrows and smiles at the gesture. If she weren't so tired, she'd probably let it bother her more, but for now, it was comforting.

The evening passed quickly. Mike's parents were a lot of fun and before long, the tension she'd been feeling slipped away.

'It's getting late.' She stifled a yawn. 'This has been lovely, but I've got to get home. Mum will have a fit when she hears about this. I don't suppose we could keep it our little secret?'

'Of course we can.' Brenda smiled. 'You're fine and there's no point getting your mother all worked up.'

'Thanks.'

After she said goodbye, Mike walked her outside to wait for her cab. He wrapped his arms around her waist and pulled her close, kissing her gently. 'You could stay the night, you know.'

'Thanks, but that wouldn't work. My mother wouldn't be happy if I didn't come home, and knowing your parents were in the next room, I wouldn't be able to sleep a wink.'

'I wasn't planning on getting any sleep,' Mike said with a chuckle.

'I definitely wouldn't be able to do that with your parents in the house!'

'Me living here — that is why you took off last night, isn't it?'

She nodded.

Mike continued, 'I don't understand why it's such a problem. They're away a lot; it just makes sense.'

'Maybe it works for you, but if it was me, I'd need my space. I could never picture myself living with my parents again under any circumstances. Don't get me wrong; I love them. I just don't want to live with them. I'd miss my privacy.'

'I suppose so. It's just that living with my parents has never really been an issue before.'

'Are you telling me that having your mum and dad in the next room has never bothered your girlfriends?'

'Since I've never brought another woman here before, it hasn't been an issue.'

Tracy was speechless. How was she supposed to respond to that? First, he'd taken her to his get-away-from-it-all spot; now he'd brought her home.

'But . . . from the way you kiss me . . . I mean, you're not . . . inexperienced,' she said, struggling to find a delicate way of expressing what she wanted to say.

'I never said I'd been a monk. I just never met anyone I cared for enough to bring them home.'

She knew she shouldn't let this discovery make her giddy inside, because she wasn't staying in Eyam, but she couldn't help it.

The cab pulled up. Standing on tiptoe, she gave Mike a quick kiss and got into the cab. She didn't let him see the huge smile on her face.

8

From the moment Tracy's cab pulled out of sight, Mike wanted to talk to her again. He kept replaying their conversation in his mind, and her comments about his living arrangements nagged at him. He glanced at his mobile phone, wanting to call her, wanting to clear the air and explain, but he wasn't sure what to say. It was more obvious than ever that if he wanted to move the relationship to the next level, it couldn't be while he lived here. But it felt too soon to tell her of the plans he'd been making.

Since he hadn't had a relationship of any kind with a woman from Eyam, he hadn't previously given much thought to where he called home. His parents travelled and he had to watch the house in their absence; living there had made sense. Since the disastrous end to their date the previous night, though, the lack of privacy and personal space was a serious issue. And since he most definitely wanted to be involved with Tracy, he knew he'd been right to try and work something out. And in the meantime, maybe they could work out a schedule and continue to see one another after she returned to London. He didn't like the city, but he could put up with it if it meant spending time with her.

Checking his watch to see how much time had elapsed since she'd left, he reached for his phone to call her and stopped when he realised he might be getting a bit ahead of himself. What was he thinking? He wanted to talk about maintaining their relationship when they hadn't even begun one, and if they were going to build a rapport, there were still too many secrets between them. For one, she hadn't explained what had happened to upset her so earlier that evening; for another, the true identity of G.L. O'Michael stood planted firmly between them. He was fairly certain that she hadn't given up her quest for the truth, but was he ready to share it? And when he did, would she be angry with him for lying to her?

Their time together amounted only to a few hours over a three-day period, but he enjoyed being with her more than he did any other woman. She challenged him on so many levels. Since he'd moved back home to take over the bookshop, his life had become too predictable — work at the shop, writing, and helping out with community events when he could. There was no excitement. The only thrill he'd allowed himself had been a two-week holiday after he'd sent his latest book to his publisher. It was something else to feel that elation right here, in his home — and feel it he did, each time he took Tracy in his arms. Whatever this was, he'd take it slow and easy; he wouldn't mind seeing where it led.

He was sure she'd be home by now,

and he hoped that whatever had sent her racing out into the wintry night hadn't flared up again. He picked up his mobile and dialled.

'Hello?' she answered in a hushed tone.

'It's me. Did I wake you?'

'No. I just don't want to wake Carrie,' she whispered.

'Sorry; I forgot how late it was and that there was a toddler in the house.'

'Don't worry about it; I'm sure she's still sound asleep. What's up?'

Mike lay back against the pillows of his bed, wanting to get comfortable. 'Nothing, really. I just wanted to make sure you got home safe.'

'Oh, how sweet,' she said, and he could hear the thinly veiled sarcasm in her voice. 'Seriously, what could possibly happen to me in Eyam?'

'Bad things happen everywhere,' he said soberly, 'even in Eyam.'

'You're right,' she said contritely. 'Thanks for checking up on me.'

'You're welcome. Did the family give

you a hard time when you got home?'

'No. Everyone was asleep, thank goodness, so I was able to sneak straight upstairs to my room. I don't want to fight with them anymore. I just wish they'd accept that I'm not moving back to Eyam.'

Despite the fact that Mike knew and respected her feelings on the matter, he still felt a twinge of disappointment.

'Are you telling me that a disagreement over your decision not to remain in Eyam is what sent you haring off into the freezing cold tonight?'

She was silent, and as the seconds ticked past he wondered if she was going to tell him the truth. He wouldn't push. He knew instinctively that she'd share her feelings when she was ready.

'More or less,' she said at last. 'I was at the bakery today, helping Susan out. Mr. White came in, said he was planning to retire, and offered to sell me his practice.'

Unfortunately, Mike knew exactly where this was going, but he listened as she related her side of the story. When she was finished, he spoke quietly. 'Tracy, you can't blame Susan for wanting her sister to come home.'

'Thanks for the support, Mike. I have to go now,' she said, her voice laced with irony.

This wasn't the way he'd envisioned this conversation. 'Hold on, Tracy — you're putting words in my mouth!'

'What, Mike? What am I missing? Do you want to tell me what a selfish, horrible person I am for wanting a life of my own?'

'No, I'm not going to say anything of the sort, and you should know I wouldn't say anything like that in the first place.' He had a feeling her overreaction to his comment and the situation in general was based on issues of misplaced guilt. 'What I mean to say is, I understand where Susan's coming from. It can't be easy raising a child alone, having her only sister so far away. My sister would love to be near me and our parents, and Mum misses them dreadfully, but the children are settled in their school and with their friends, so it's the sacrifice she makes.'

'I'm sorry to hear that, Mike, but I'm not your sister. At the moment I don't have a burning need to be in Eyam — family or no family.'

'Ouch! That's telling me. No, you're not my sister; otherwise, those kisses yesterday and earlier tonight would have been highly inappropriate.' He smiled when he heard her giggle, as he'd hoped she would. He took her laughter as a good sign and continued. 'From what I've seen, Susan hardly socialises at all since she had Carrie, and I'm sure she's lonely. Wanting her sister nearby isn't such a difficult thing to understand, surely?'

As he pleaded Susan's case, he realised he wanted the same thing. It made it easy to inject sincerity in his words. He'd like nothing better than for Tracy to come home and take over Mr. White's practice. He hoped she was thinking about what he'd said, because she'd been quiet an awfully long time. He felt relief when he heard her voice again.

'I suppose Susan has a point, but her feelings aren't mine, and I have a right to my opinions too. I grew up under Mum's vigilant, over-protective eye. I couldn't do anything for fear I'd get hurt or sick, and I let her control my life. Susan rebelled against Mum's treatment and risked punishment for a life of her own. I wasn't strong enough to stand up to Mum the way she did. I think it's that lack of self-assurance which made school so painful for me; I had to leave Eyam to find myself.' She stopped talking, but he didn't say anything because he had a feeling there was more to come. 'I can't come back and live under the microscope lens of a small village. Can you understand that?'

'I think I can, but you have to realise you're not that shy teenager anymore either. You're a strong, confident woman. You'd be fine anywhere, including Eyam. As the expression goes, 'you've come a long way, baby.' ' You can do whatever you want to do.'

'Thanks for the vote of confidence.' She laughed, but it wasn't the joyful laughter he loved. 'I've got to go; I'm tired, and it's been a long day.'

'Before you hang up, I want to ask you something.'

'Go ahead. My saviour should be entitled to ask a question.'

'Will you come to the fair with me tomorrow?'

'I'd like to, but I promised Carrie I'd take her to see Santa and watch the tree lighting ceremony.'

'You can do both. The party for the grown-ups doesn't start until nine o'clock. You have plenty of time to spend with Carrie. I'll be busy during the day anyway; I'm helping out until about eight.'

'In that case, I'd love to go to the fair with you.'

'Wonderful. Good night, Tracy. Sweet dreams.'

'Good night, Mike.'

* * *

The conversation with Mike haunted her sleep, especially the fact that she'd put herself in danger running from her family instead of staying and confronting the issue the way an adult would. Hadn't she learned that you had to face issues to overcome them? In fact, hadn't she done the same thing years ago — run away instead of dealing with things? She'd left Eyam and refused to look back. Oh, she kept in touch with her family, but she'd rarely initiated the conversations — missed making the calls, almost never booked the tickets; no, if her mother hadn't insisted on regular contact, she'd have let it all go. Why? She loved her family, and absolutely worshipped Carrie. Would returning to Eyam be so terrible? she wondered as she tossed and turned.

She'd worked incredibly hard to get where she was; was she willing to give up her chance at a partnership in London and the prestige she had working for such a large, well-respected firm? She'd put in too many hours to throw it all away, and for what? A small practice in Eyam? Even if it meant being closer to her family, was it too steep a price to pay?

Her thoughts turned to Mike. Coming back to Eyam would mean being closer to him, to the man who'd dropped whatever he was doing and had rushed to rescue her. She hadn't even considered he might be busy when she'd asked for help. If he hadn't called again, she would have. How selfish was that? Had she always put herself first like this? All right, she had been well and truly lost, and with the light fading and the temperature rapidly dropping, she'd been more than a little frightened, but since she'd come home, she'd started to look at her 'me first' philosophy in a whole new way. Yes, she'd left, pursued her dream, and had worked her backside off. In Eyam she'd been lost, in danger of suffocating, but where was she now? Her guilt and shame at being so selfish weighed heavily on her, but she couldn't come back; she just couldn't.

She thought back to her decision to leave and realised how difficult it must have been for the rest of her family. Her mother, mollycoddling as she'd been, had wanted her to stay close to home, go to a local university the way Susan planned to do, and she'd almost given in — would have, if it hadn't been for her dad. He must have heard her muffled tears that night after yet another argument with her mother, and had come into her room. He'd said that she needed to do what her heart told her to do, and with that advice in mind, she had. It was the credo that continued to drive her life, but now she was no longer sure what her heart was telling her.

One thing Mike had said had planted itself firmly in her mind, and she resolved to act on it. Susan was lonely, and she needed to socialise. He'd invited Tracy to the fair tomorrow and she was pretty sure, based on his eloquent defence of her sister tonight, he wouldn't mind if Susan came along. It would be fun and there was a good chance she might be able to find someone with more than a passing interest in her beautiful sister. Yes, that was what she would do — find a man for Susan.

Tracy would have been the first one to tell you that having a man in your life didn't guarantee happiness, but in Susan's case having someone to share her burdens might be exactly what she needed. And if she had a life of her own, she might be more understanding of Tracy's need to have one too. Since Susan refused to discuss Carrie's dad, Tracy would find a man for her who could fit that role too. Tracy felt better about her new mission and settled down to sleep. Tomorrow was going to be a busy day.

★　★　★

Despite the late night and her unsettled thoughts, Tracy was up early the following morning — although not as early as Susan, who'd already left for the bakery. Tracy took her opportunity and started to put her plan into action.

'Mum, would you mind watching Carrie later tonight?' Tracy asked.

'Of course not. Why?'

'I'd like to take Susan to the fair.'

Her mother laughed. 'Good luck with that; Susan hasn't been to the fair since Carrie was born. Come to think of it, she rarely goes anywhere other than work.' Her mother paused, and Tracy could see the lines of worry etched on her mother's face.

'Susan used to be such a social butterfly, but since she's become a mother she's become so serious. Her friends used to call, but she said no all the time, and eventually they stopped calling. Susan never complains, but she must be going a little stir crazy.'

'Don't worry, Mum. I'll take her out and we'll have a great time.'

'I hope so; it would do her good to have some fun.'

'Wish me luck.' She kissed her mother goodbye and headed to the bakery, hoping Susan wasn't still upset about yesterday.

★　★　★

Sweet Buns was usually closed on Sundays, but because of the Christmas holiday Susan had decided to open the bakery for half a day, like many of the other shops in the village. It was as busy, if not busier, than it had been the previous day. Susan looked up when the bell chimed, and the relief on her face had Tracy feeling guilty.

'Thank goodness you're here!' Susan looked as if she were about to collapse.

'Really? Why?' Tracy inquired, realising full well exactly what Susan was about to ask. She decided to use her sister's need as a bargaining chip. After all, it was for her own good.

'Would you mind giving me a hand

again today? Just for a little while. Please? I'm swamped.'

'Gladly, but you have to agree to come to the fair with me tonight.'

Susan stopped mid-step and turned on her. 'What? I can't do that. I have Carrie.'

Tracy placed her hands on her hips, her face dead serious. 'I've taken care of that. Mum's agreed to watch her. If you want my help, you have to say yes.'

Tracy was taken aback when it became obvious that her words had somehow hurt her sister. She was confused by Susan's reaction. 'Susan,' she went on, 'it's only the fair. It's a chance to have some fun. It isn't as if I'm asking you to jump off a cliff.'

'Fine. I'll go. Wash your hands, grab an apron, and give me a hand.'

Tracy smiled and hurried to do as she'd been told. The first part of her plan had worked. For step two, she needed to speak to Mike. With any luck, he'd be able to rustle up a friend who'd be interested in an old-fashioned double date.

The shop was busy, but as they'd closed early, her feet didn't hurt as much as they had yesterday. As she watched Susan lock up the shop, she found that she'd enjoyed her manic time waitressing. Now, she was looking forward to quality time with her favourite niece.

'I'll be home shortly,' she told Susan. 'I have a stop to make.'

'Okay. I'll have Carrie ready when you get there.'

One of the things Tracy loved best about Susan was her ability to let go of things. The disagreement from yesterday afternoon was forgotten and hadn't caused any tension between them today. That was her sister's way — she said her piece and didn't hold a grudge.

Tracy smiled and headed over to her bike, then parked on the next street. She had someone to see before going home.

9

Tracy walked towards the park, where she saw several people putting the finishing touches to Santa's grotto. The gigantic chair sat in a half-building with sides and a back, but no front wall. Children would line up later today for a chance to sit on Santa's knee and whisper their Christmas wishes. While they did, eager teenagers dressed as elves would take photographs and print them for proud parents. She was excited at the prospect of seeing Carrie's first encounter with Santa.

The park looked incredible — fairy lights, a huge real pine tree waiting for the final decorations, games, a beer tent, a special shopping area where children could shop for Mum and Dad, as well as a children's arts-and-crafts table. The stage was waiting for the local talent that would entertain throughout the festivities. After the official opening, there'd be a DJ playing music for the rest of the evening. They'd got a lot done since she'd walked by five hours earlier.

Mike had mentioned he'd be helping set up again today, so she knew he'd be here and not at the bookshop. Tonight the Christmas tree lights would be switched on and, all afternoon until dark, children could place baubles and other decorations on the tree.

She was sure Mike would be easy to spot. His physique was emblazoned on her mind, and she knew she'd be able to pick him out of a crowd. After her personal late-night battle, she'd determined to try to curb her selfishness, and felt she needed to run her decision to invite Susan by him — he deserved to know ahead of time, especially if she wanted him to get her sister a date.

As she'd expected, her eyes found him amidst the other volunteers right away. He was helping lay the wooden flooring that would serve as a dance floor later. He had his back to her, and she watched as the muscles on his shoulders bunched to handle the weight of a section. He must have sensed her watching him because his gaze found her, and he smiled. Her breath caught at the sight of him. His hair was damp with sweat, and he must have run his fingers through it several times for it to be in such disarray; hers itched to do the same. Without giving herself time to think of the consequences, she walked right up to him and kissed him. He was irresistible, and she forgot herself in the moment, until she heard the others nearby wolf-whistling.

Breathless, somewhat overcome by her boldness, but unwilling to show how her loss of self-control bothered her, she gave the onlookers a shy smile. Mike laughed.

'Do we get one too?' asked a man she recognised, but whose name she couldn't remember.

'Sorry lads, this one is all mine,' said Mike, smiling down at her.

Tracy's heart constricted at his claim and she couldn't stop the huge smile that spread across her face.

'I'm all yours, am I?' she teased.

'Yes, you are.' The look in his eyes dared her to deny it.

'Okay,' she uttered, suddenly shy, and her heart beat as if she'd just finished a marathon. He pulled her more closely into his body. She forgot about everyone and everything except Mike.

It had been a long time since any man had laid claim to her publicly like this. The last man to do so had been Chris, her first boyfriend. She'd met him shortly after she'd arrived in London. She'd been lucky enough to land a waitressing job in a bar to earn the money she needed for tuition. Lonely as she'd been, being with him had been comforting. He'd helped her through the transition from shy village girl to the self-sufficient woman she was today. He'd introduced her to fast cars and even faster bikes and, although the romance between them had fizzled, they'd remained good friends. In many ways, he was the brother she'd never had.

She pulled away from Mike. 'I need to talk to you for a minute.'

'I'd rather keep kissing you, but okay. What's up?' He grinned mischievously.

She took his arm and moved him away from the rest of the men who were finishing off the dance floor. 'I paid attention to what you said last night about Susan. Would you mind if she joined us tonight? I want her to have some fun while I'm here.'

'No, of course I don't mind. Instead of escorting one beautiful woman, I'll have two. I'll be the envy of every man in Eyam.' He gave her a quick kiss to punctuate his statement.

'Brilliant. You wouldn't happen to have a friend you could bring along for her, would you?'

'Let me get this straight. You want me to arrange a blind date for your sister?' There was more than a little confusion and concern in his voice.

'Yes.'

Mike frowned. 'Do you think that's a good idea?'

'Probably not. I'm sure she'll be annoyed at first, maybe even furious, but I know Susan. She might not be over the moon at being set up, but she won't make a scene, and eventually, she'll have fun . . . I hope! Just make sure you bring someone with a sense of humour.'

He laughed. 'It's your funeral. Don't be surprised if she tries to get even with you for this.'

'Very funny. Do you know someone who might fit the bill or not?'

'Actually, I have a friend who just got back to the village. Do you remember Jeremy Barrett?'

'The name sounds familiar, but I can't picture him.'

'Good, then I know he's not competition. Jeremy left me a text asking what I was up to tonight, so I don't think he's got plans. I'll give him a call as soon as I'm done here.'

'Wonderful!' She couldn't contain her excitement. She stood on her tiptoes to give him a quick kiss. 'I have to go now. I'll see you later.'

'I like the sound of that,' he said and smiled at her.

She waved and headed towards her bike, looking back once to take in the glorious sight of Mike hard at work.

* * *

Tracy followed in Susan's wake, watching her carry an exhausted Carrie up the stairs. The comatose child still clutched the stuffed snowman she'd won at the snowball-tossing game that had been set up for the smaller children. Exhausted by all the excitement, she hadn't even made it to the car before falling asleep.

The afternoon and early evening had been wonderful, and Tracy had felt like a child again herself. Her entire family had gone to the celebration together. Local talent had taken turns entertaining the crowd. There'd been a magician and a puppet show for the kids as well as a sing-along for Christmas carols, and it seemed as if everyone in the village had turned up for the occasion. Watching Carrie dance around with the other toddlers, making up their own version of the lyrics, had Tracy joining them on the dance floor. She loved being with her and knew she'd miss her terribly when the time came for her to leave.

She'd taken her niece shopping for a present for Mummy, and Tracy had purchased a bag of magical reindeer food for Carrie to spread on the lawn on Christmas Eve to make sure Santa and the reindeer didn't miss her house. The little bag filled with oatmeal, cinnamon, cloves, and star glitter was a huge success, and every child in Eyam no doubt had one.

Carrie had hung four ornaments on the tree — two baubles, an angel, and a toy soldier. When they'd finished with the tree-decorating they'd stopped at the craft table to make a Santa face using paper plates, cotton balls, and almost an entire small jar of white glue. Grandma had taken the gooey treasure and proclaimed it the best Santa face of the lot. Tracy was certain that, by this time tomorrow, it would have a place of honour amidst all the rest of the Stewart Christmas paraphernalia.

Then it had been time to go and see Santa. Carrie had been so excited about the prospect of sitting on Santa's knee that she could hardly stand still, and that excitement had lasted right up until the moment when the toddler finally got to the head of the queue. One 'Ho, ho, ho,' and she burst into tears and tried to crawl up her mother's body! The tears raged until Tracy agreed to sit on Santa's knee too. When Carrie realised there were sweets involved though, the tears subsided!

They had hot chocolate and sugar-coated biscuits, hot dogs, and messy candy floss that might leave a permanent pink stain on the bib Susan had been prepared enough to bring with her. Tracy couldn't remember the last time she'd eaten so much. At dusk the mayor flipped the switches, turning on the thousands of coloured twinkling lights that festooned every stand, tent and tree in the village square. The Christmas tree itself, aglow with hundreds of white lights, was beautiful and Carrie's reaction when all the lights were turned on was worth every exhausting second of the day. Tracy wouldn't have missed this for anything!

The day had been almost perfect; the only thing that would have made it better would have been to have Mike there to share Carrie's excitement. Visions of a little girl with green eyes and dark hair swam in front of her eyes, as she pictured a child of her own at the fair. She gave herself a shake. Where had that idea come from?

Tracy thought she'd seen Mike a couple of times during the day, but he'd always been busy with something. A fair like this one was built on the backs of community-minded volunteers like him, and all of them had done a wonderful job.

Susan had carried her snoozing daughter to the car as final preparations were being made to turn the children's celebration into a celebration for adults and teens. They'd have an hour to get ready before meeting Mike and his friend. Tracy could hardly wait.

She hurried to her room to change and put on the clothes she'd planned to wear. She regretted not bringing some of her snazzier outfits, but the last thing she'd expected to do in Eyam was meet someone, let alone someone who was starting to really matter to her.

Since returning to the house, Susan had tried more than once to persuade Tracy to go without her, and Tracy was sure she'd give it a few more attempts before they left to meet Mike.

Downstairs her parents were settling in for a night of TV and babysitting, although Carrie was so tired it was doubtful she'd wake before morning. Tracy was excited. In all the years that she'd lived in Eyam and gone to the annual winter fair, this was the first time she'd done so as a grown woman with a date. The butterflies in her stomach were doing handstands, and a permanent smile was plastered on her face.

*　*　*

Mike stood in the shower letting the hot water pound onto him. He'd had a very busy couple of days, and by the time he'd got home every muscle in his body ached. The only thing that kept him from collapsing exhausted on the bed was the thought of Tracy — and the future he had started to imagine for them.

Yesterday, prompted by Tracy's obviously negative reaction to discovering he lived in the same house as his parents, he'd stopped by a local estate agent to see what houses were for sale in the surrounding area. Once the seed had been planted, the need for his own place had taken root. It had become clear to him over the past couple of days that he wanted a relationship with Tracy, and while he could travel to London, he hoped he'd be able to convince her to come home to see him too. Judging by the conversation he'd had with her last night, he knew he'd done the right thing to start the ball rolling on getting a place of his own — even though he'd hesitated to spring that bit of news on her just yet. He'd been surprised at how quickly he'd found what he believed to be the perfect place for him — for them. It was just outside the village on the verge of the Peaks, private, but still close enough to civilisation. The back garden had a spectacular view. He'd loved it, and he was sure she would too.

Every time he thought about his future, he pictured Tracy in it. Why that was, he didn't really understand, but he knew he was deeply attracted to her. He kept trying to reason with himself, tell himself that he was setting himself up for a fall, but his heart refused to listen. Tracy was fiercely independent, a woman he'd known less than a handful of days, and here he was looking at houses with her in mind. He was worse than his mother, planning fairy-tale weddings with a girl he barely knew, but the connection they shared was real and deep, and he hoped she felt the same way. It hurt too much to think she might just be playing with him while she was here.

He thought about what she'd said about her family, Susan in particular, wanting her to come home. Starting tonight, he'd be adding his not-so-subtle pleas to theirs. He wanted to make it as hard for her to leave him as it would be for him to see her go.

★ ★ ★

Mike was a few minutes early. He scanned the crowd looking for Jeremy, who'd agreed to meet him by the 'This way to the North Pole' sign. Jeremy had been hesitant about coming out with them tonight until Mike had mentioned Susan, then he'd been all for it — not that he blamed him. Susan was a beautiful woman, but she wasn't the sister for him.

He spotted Jeremy walking towards him, and not too far behind he saw Tracy and Susan, but she could have been alone for all the attention he paid to any other person there. She was beautiful, with her hair shining and flickering in the thousands of lights strung around the square. She wore a black knitted top under her leather jacket, and a pair of black skinny jeans hugged every inch of her exquisite curves.

She looked up at him and smiled shyly. The woman was such a contradiction. Most of the time she was confident and feisty, but every so often he got a glimpse of a softer, more vulnerable side of her that made him want to wrap his arms around her and protect her from the world.

'Mike!' Jeremy said, breaking into his thoughts and severing his connection to the approaching beauty.

Mike reached for Jeremy's extended hand, and wrapped his arm around his friend; he hadn't seen him since he'd been home on leave almost three years ago for his father's funeral. It was good to see him home safe and sound. When Jeremy had joined the army, Mike had worried about him, but Jeremy had always been restless, the adventure-seeking kind, and the army had seemed like a good fit for him at the time.

'Glad you could make it,' Mike said, giving him another squeeze before letting go.

'Thanks; glad to be here. Where are the lovely ladies?'

'Right behind you,' Mike answered, forcing his friend to turn around.

Mike pointed towards them, but the second Susan's eyes locked on them the smile on her face disappeared, and she froze.

'Come on,' Jeremy said, slapping him on the back and heading towards the girls, apparently quite eager to meet his date.

Mike laughed at his friend's enthusiasm and followed him. As they neared, he realised that Susan and Tracy were having a heated discussion, which was what he'd expected would happen when Susan realised that Tracy had set her up; but as soon as they were within earshot the girls stopped talking. He kissed Tracy quickly, and then stood back to admire her.

'Tracy, this is Jeremy Barrett. Jeremy, this is Tracy Stewart.' They shook hands.

'Nice to meet you, Jeremy.'

'You too.' He turned his attention to Susan. Mike thought Susan had paled substantially. He was no expert, but she looked ready to pass out. Before he could make even a quasi-introduction, Jeremy spoke.

'Hello, Susan. You look great.'

Mike could feel the waves of tension rolling off them. He was sure Tracy felt it too because her arm tightened slightly around him.

'I have to go.' Susan turned and ran through the crowd.

Tracy unwrapped herself from Mike, and without a word, took off after her sister.

Mike looked over at Jeremy. 'What on earth just happened?' He was confused. This wasn't the date he'd hoped for.

'Beats me,' Jeremy answered, shrugging his shoulders, but he was still watching the place where Susan had stood, and the look on his face said he knew exactly what had happened.

10

'You didn't tell me you knew Susan,' Mike accused. 'And from the look on her face and the way she scarpered out of here, it's obvious that she doesn't want to know you. What happened?'

'Nothing, as far as I know.' There was a strange defensiveness to his tone that made Mike wonder whether or not Jeremy really had been as surprised by her sudden flight as Mike had.

'Well, this is becoming a familiar pattern, and it isn't one I like. I'm getting rather sick of being left cooling my heels on my own,' grumbled Mike, running a hand through his hair. 'It seems I spend more time watching Tracy walk away from me than I do watching her approach.' He shook his head. 'I'm not letting her walk out of here without an explanation. Whatever bee Susan has in her bonnet about you shouldn't be enough for Tracy to disappear like this.'

'Well at least she said hello,' said a disconsolate Jeremy. 'Susan turned and ran the minute she set eyes on me!'

Maybe he was being unreasonable, but Mike had been anticipating this moment all day, and watching Tracy disappear after her sister without so much as a word left him more than a little disappointed. He looked at Jeremy standing beside him, staring after the girls. By the look on his face, he'd been sucker-punched too. Clearly he and Susan had a history, and from the looks of it, the relationship hadn't ended well. It would have been helpful if he'd mentioned that earlier when Mike had asked him to come along tonight.

Mike scanned the crowd, looking in the direction the girls had fled. He could barely see Tracy amidst the sea of partygoers who'd turned out for the grand opening ceremony and the ensuing festivities. He wasn't about to let her leave him like this. So what if

Susan was less than happy about being set up? That was her problem, not theirs. Fleeing as if the hounds of hell were in pursuit was hardly adult behaviour, but it seemed to be a characteristic the sisters shared.

Tracy might be concerned about her sister's reaction, but chasing after her on her own, basically shutting him out, frustrated him. He'd warned her that this might happen — well maybe not this, exactly, but he'd told her Susan might be angry and annoyed. Who wouldn't be? He remembered his own irritation years ago when his sister was constantly doing the same to him, but this time he and Tracy were in it together. Was this just another excuse for her to leave him high and dry? She wouldn't stay with him because his parents were there; she wouldn't come back to Eyam because she had her own life; she left him because her sister fled. Exasperated, he started to walk in her direction. Was he the only one who wanted to see this relationship go somewhere?

'Come on,' he said to Jeremy. 'She's not going to leave me hanging like this again.' The two men started after the women, their long strides covering the ground quickly.

He thought of her kiss today; it had been warm and spontaneous, and he knew it had affected her. He'd seen it as them staking their claim on one another. Clearly he'd been wrong. It hadn't meant anything to her. Well, he wasn't to be toyed with and then thrown aside if something better came up. He moved swiftly through the crowd, eating up the distance between them. He needed to set things straight with her, once and for all.

★   ★   ★

'Susan! Susan, wait!' Tracy ran flat out, dodging people as she did, trying to catch up with her sister, who seemed to be running as if her life depended on it.

What had just happened? Mike had warned her that Susan might be put out about being set up tonight, but she hadn't expected her to behave this way. Susan had been really upset, much more than Tracy would have expected, and she'd been rude. If there was one thing Susan never was, it was rude. Running away was her coping strategy, not Susan's. What was Susan running from? It was only a date, for goodness' sake.

She saw Susan up ahead, slowing as she approached the car park, and she put on an extra push to catch up to her before she reached the car. If Susan got there first, she'd probably take off and leave Tracy stranded, without an explanation for what had happened and feeling like a fool — she hated feeling that way. Closing in on her, Tracy reached out and grabbed her sister's arm before she could escape again.

'What's wrong with you?' she panted. 'What exactly is your problem?'

Winded, she breathed heavily, surprised she'd been able to say that much. What she wanted to do was throw herself to the ground until the stitch in her side vanished and the burning in her leg muscles subsided, or clasp her sister the way people who'd finished a marathon did, but she knew enough not to try that. Something in her posture said that would be a huge mistake. Tracy leaned against the nearest car for support, grateful that it was an older model without one of those touch-activated anti-theft devices. All she needed now was a blaring alarm to attract even more attention to them.

Susan turned towards her and Tracy took a step back, stunned by the anger in her sister's face and the steady stream of tears flowing down her cheeks.

'What were you thinking Tracy?' Susan cried, her voice filled with distress. 'Do you have any idea what you've done?'

'Susan, what are you talking about?'

she asked, confusion and guilt warring within her. She knew her cheeks had reddened in deadly contrast to Susan's pale ones. Her sister looked scared to death. 'I just thought . . . '

Her sister cut her off. 'No, you didn't think. That's your problem — you never think!' The fury in Susan's voice felt like a slap in the face. Tracy had never heard her sister so angry.

'I'm sorry. I thought a little fun was a good idea. I shouldn't have sprung this on you the way I did. I shouldn't have set you up without your permission. I was wrong, and I'm sorry.'

Susan's eyes focused on something behind Tracy. 'I have to go — now!' There was no mistaking the look of horror on Susan's face. Tracy turned to see what had caused the panic and saw Mike and Jeremy quickly approaching them. She knew Mike wasn't responsible for her sister's terror, which meant it must be Jeremy.

Tracy put two and two together and realised that it wasn't being set up that had caused the panic. It was Jeremy himself. Susan was scared stiff of him. She and Mike had made a huge mistake. She didn't really know this man, but her sister's reaction made her stomach sink. Jeremy and Susan clearly had a history, and something about him left her sister petrified.

Every protective instinct she had went on high alert. Tracy grabbed Susan's hand and raced towards the car. She knew her behaviour would concern Mike, especially since she'd just looked him in the eye, but she'd explain later, once her sister was safe. At the moment, getting Susan home before she passed out took precedence over everything else.

She'd just pushed Susan into the passenger seat of the car knowing her sister couldn't possibly drive as distraught as she was, and was rounding the boot to get to the driver's side when someone grabbed her shoulder, and she screamed.

'Calm down, for goodness' sake. It's

me. Where do you think you're going?'
Mike asked, every bit as angry as Susan
had been, but Tracy couldn't worry
about that now. Susan was in danger of
hyperventilating, and she had to get her
calmed down and home as soon as
possible. She'd explain everything to
him on the phone later.

'Susan isn't feeling well,' she
answered quickly. It wasn't the full
truth, but it wasn't a complete lie
either. 'I'm going to take her home. I'll
call you later.' She moved closer to
give him a goodbye kiss, but he
stepped away from her.

'What's the matter?' she asked,
confused, realising just how angry and
upset he was.

'I can't continue like this, Tracy.' He
ran his hand through his hair in that
adorable way he did when he was
frustrated or nervous. She watched with
mixed feelings as he paced beside her.
She knew instinctively that whatever he
was going to say would hurt.

'You blow hot and cold; I never know

where I stand with you. I'd hoped that we could make this attraction between us work, but I really don't think we can. I like you Tracy, I like you a lot, more than any other woman I've known, and I think we could have a future together despite the fact that we haven't known each other long. But there's too much drama here. There's always something with you. I can't keep standing by watching you dash off without a decent explanation. I can't do this — no, I won't do this.'

Anger replaced the hurt his words had caused, and her fury bubbled over.

'What are you talking about? What relationship? We've known each other four days, for heaven's sake. I came here to spend Christmas with my family, not to get involved in a happily-ever-after relationship with anyone. I'm not staying here. I never said I was. Goodbye, Mike. If you'll excuse me, I have to get my sister home.'

She turned on her heel and got into

the car before he could see the tears in her eyes and the crushed look on her face. She looked over at Susan, sitting stone-like, staring straight ahead as Jeremy drew nearer, a kicked-puppy look on his face.

Tracy closed the door before Mike could do or say anything and started the car. She put it in gear and slowly eased out of the parking bay. When she looked in the rear view mirror, she saw both men standing where she'd left them, watching the car as she drove away. Susan didn't say a word, but sobs racked her body. Tracy drove carefully through the blur of her own tears, grateful when she saw the familiar driveway of home.

★　★　★

'Back already?' her mother called from the living room as Tracy followed Susan into the house.

Grateful she hadn't got up and come through to the hall to see their tear-stained faces, Tracy answered for them both, hoping that just this once her mum wouldn't realise she was lying.

'There were too many teenagers, and the park was rammed. I didn't realise how tiring working in the bakery two days in a row could be. I can't imagine how Susan does it every day. We decided not to bother and called it a night. I'm going to bed. Susan's already gone up. I'll see you in the morning.'

Completely engrossed in the crime drama she was watching, her mother mumbled a good night, and Tracy rushed up the stairs before she changed her mind. She wasn't ready for the inquisition just yet. She wasn't even sure she understood herself what had happened tonight. She went upstairs and stood outside Susan's door. Her sister's muffled tears sounded loud in her ears. She headed back to her room to shed a few of her own.

Tracy lay in bed exhausted after her crying jag, ironically aware that she'd cried more since coming home than she had in years. As she lay there, she realised the half-truth in the words she'd said to Mike. She hadn't come home looking to fall in love — but it had happened, and now the heartache she felt was something else she'd have to deal with. It was for the best. She only had a few more days here, then she was leaving and not looking back. Her life wasn't in Eyam, it was in London, and the possibility that he'd move for her was non-existent. What kind of relationship could you really have that far apart?

Tomorrow was Christmas Eve, and with it came all the Stewart traditions she loved. She couldn't allow her feelings for any man to come between her and her family's happiness. This was her first Christmas home in years, and possibly her last. She wasn't going to let her wayward heart ruin it.

First things first, she'd have to mend her fences with Susan. What she'd done, regardless of her intentions, had been thoughtless and inconsiderate.

She pushed aside her own sadness, got up, and headed to Susan's room. It was almost eleven, and the house was dark. That meant Mum and Dad had gone to bed, so they'd have to keep their voices low.

She knocked softly on Susan's door, but got no response. Maybe she'd fallen asleep. She opened the door to check just in case Susan was purposefully ignoring her. If she could, she wanted to fix this now, not let it fester until morning.

'Susan?'

'Go away, Tracy,' she mumbled. Tracy was surprised to realise that she was still crying. Surely no man, no matter what he'd done, could be worth this much anguish?

'No, I'm not going anywhere until you explain to me what happened tonight. You need to tell me what's going on.'

'Oh, right,' Susan replied, anger replacing her anguish, 'you're not going anywhere! That's rich! The minute

Christmas is over, you're going to drive out of here on that fancy bike of yours, leaving us all wondering if you're ever coming back. And just like the last time, you'll leave me here to clean up your mess.'

Tracy stepped into the room and closed the door softly behind her. She didn't want to wake up the rest of the house, but this discussion had definitely not gone the way she'd planned.

'Clean up what mess? What are you talking about? You're not making any sense.'

'You may be a high-flying lawyer, but you can be so clueless. Ten years ago you left home and left me, your little sister, here. You never looked back. Do you have any idea what Mum and Dad went through every week when you didn't call; what a state Mum was in? Every time you made another excuse not to come home I had to listen to Mum crying and Dad trying to console her, even though his heart was breaking too. And what about me? You didn't give two hoots what happened to me!'

Tracy felt her own frustration rise. Not this again! 'I'm not going to apologise for building a life for myself! Ever since I got home, it seems all I've been doing is defending my decisions, my right to my life and my dreams, and I'm sick of it. I'm going to stay until after Christmas, but after that, I'm going back to London just as I'd planned. I'm sorry you can't understand and appreciate that. Good night.' Knowing that she wouldn't be able to fix the problem that existed between them with an apology, now or ever, she turned towards the door to return to her room.

'Tracy?' Susan's small voice small made Tracy turn and look at her.

'What?' All the hurt and anguish she'd felt all evening was just below the surface. She was on the verge of tears again thinking of everything she'd lost.

'Jeremy is Carrie's father.'

★ ★ ★

Mike was beginning to think he'd lost his mind. In a matter of minutes he'd gone from being excited at the prospect of spending a few hours in Tracy's company to being distraught, knowing he might never hold her in his arms again. He watched as the car disappeared into the distance.

'I'm not in the mood for this,' he said, indicating the fair behind him. Jeremy stood there, staring into the night, looking as if he'd been kicked.

'Neither am I,' Jeremy answered, 'but I could use a drink. Let's go to the Queen's Head.'

★   ★   ★

'I just don't understand her,' Mike said, his third beer giving him the courage to voice his frustration. Usually a pint or two calmed him, but tonight the alcohol seemed to have the opposite effect. Sitting here in relative silence, next to his old friend who looked as bewildered and confused as he felt, just added to his irritation and edginess.

'I can't help you, mate. Sorry. I haven't a clue. When it comes to women, the only conclusion I've come to over the years is that men aren't meant to understand them — ever. They are complicated creatures whose reasoning powers defy logic.'

Mike raised his glass in a salute. 'You can say that again. I haven't had a lot of experience with women, it's true, and the ones I usually spend time with are uncomplicated. With Tracy it's different — and she's driving me mad!'

Jeremy sat there with an annoying smirk on his face. 'You've got it bad, haven't you?' he hooted. Mike felt tempted to wipe the smile off his face, but, although he definitely felt the alcohol he'd consumed on an empty stomach, he wasn't drunk enough to pick a fight with a trained military man. Instead, he took another mouthful of beer.

'Not anymore. The lady isn't interested.'

'Maybe it isn't all women. Maybe it's just the Stewart sisters who are hard to understand.' Jeremy took a drink. Mike noticed a hardness about him he hadn't seen before.

'What do you know about the Stewart sisters? You've been gone a long time.'

Jeremy snorted without humour. 'I don't know anything about Tracy, but I thought I knew Susan. Clearly I was wrong.' His eyes became distant as he took another swig of his beer, and Mike saw pain there.

'When did you meet Susan? It can't have been in school. She'd have been way too young for you then.'

Mike didn't think he was going to answer, and his curiosity was piqued enough that, for the moment, he set his own pain aside. Jeremy was quiet, lost in thought, and from the sad look on his face, if he wasn't willing to answer that would be okay.

'When I came home to bury Dad I was a wreck. I made some bad decisions, bad choices, and Susan helped me get my head on straight. We spent time together. I didn't hear from her again but even though it's been three years or so, I thought we'd shared something special. I thought she'd be pleased to see me. I was obviously wrong. I mean, she took off as soon as she saw me; she couldn't even say hello. Women, hey — who needs them?'

The haunted look in his friend's eyes gave the lie to his half-hearted joke. Mike didn't push him.

'Yes,' he said, raising his glass in a toast. 'It must just be the Stewart women. Good luck to any poor fool who falls in love with either one of them.'

They clinked their glasses together in camaraderie, and Mike knew damn well that they were the fools who needed the luck. Instead of going home as he probably should, he ordered another round. He wasn't driving and neither was Jeremy. The beer was cold and tasted good. The night was going to be a long one as it was. No point in starting it any earlier than he had to.

* * *

Mike regretted his decision to stay at the bar until closing time. His head throbbed and he opted to walk to work in the morning, hoping it would clear his head. Despite the one too many beers he'd had, instead of the oblivion of a drunken stupor, his night had been plagued with images of Tracy. At one point he'd wanted to go over to Tracy's house and have it out with her, but mercifully Jeremy had talked him out of it. That in itself had been a strange turn of events, since in the past Mike had been the voice of reason.

As he walked by Sweet Buns, he could see the place was already bustling. No doubt the sisters had had a good night's sleep, and that irritated him even more. Usually he loved every minute he spent in the bookshop, but today he just wanted to get as far away from this place and its memories of Tracy as he could.

It was Christmas Eve, and he was miserable. In his naïveté, he'd pictured this day very differently. He stared at the package he'd wrapped yesterday — signed copies of his Detective Rick Foster series, books he'd intended to give Tracy as a Christmas present. He'd planned to reveal the truth to her tonight when he gave her the gift, hoping that with this last barrier gone between them, they could start a relationship that could lead to happily-ever-after. Who was he trying to kid — they'd never even had happily-for-now! While he'd been taking down barriers, she'd been building brick walls. At least they'd called it quits before he'd divulged his secret to her and ruined his own life. Once the people of Eyam knew he was G.L. O'Michael, he'd have no peace. He looked at the clock. Today was a half-day for him, since he'd promised to help with the second half of the children's fair this afternoon. He needed coffee, strong coffee.

Headache more or less gone, but still feeling the after-effects of his self-induced alcohol poisoning, he locked up the shop at noon and headed down the street to the square. He spent the afternoon helping entertain the children until the fair closed at four. He'd hoped being surrounded by Christmas cheer would dispel his gloominess, but he'd kept scanning the crowd for Tracy, and felt worse now than he had earlier. He'd seen Susan lock up Sweet Buns a couple of hours ago and thought she might come back with Carrie, but she hadn't.

He meant what he'd told Tracy last night. He just hadn't expected it would turn out like this. It was true he couldn't keep chasing after her, and it was her turn to make a move. But what if she didn't? What if he'd let his pride get in the way and he'd lost it all? He walked home, replaying everything that had happened in his mind, and realised that he might have made a huge error in judgement.

★ ★ ★

Christmas Eve tea in the O'Neill household was a disaster. His parents felt the absence of their daughter and grandchildren, and even though they'd just come back from a two-week visit and had Skyped for over an hour, his mother's long face brought them all down. To make matters worse, Mum had somehow learned of his falling-out with Tracy and wanted answers from him about what had gone wrong, but he couldn't give her the answers she wanted because he didn't have them himself.

Mike locked himself in his office, determined to forget everything for a few hours, lost in the world of Rick Foster; but when Rick's new love interest walked into the story, he realised she was Tracy on paper. He knew that what he'd said last night wasn't going to be enough. He needed to finish this once and for all. Obviously she didn't want him. She'd had all day to phone him and hadn't. The emotions that had plagued him all day, making him miserable, clearly hadn't bothered her at all.

He saved his file, shut down his computer, and went to the bathroom. He needed to get the last of the hangover's sluggishness out of his body. He stepped into the shower, allowing the water to ease the tiredness out of his muscles, and trying to clear his mind — but thoughts of Tracy just wouldn't leave him in peace. He smacked his forehead on the shower wall in frustration. The woman was driving him mad! He turned the water from hot to cold in an effort to clear his mind. Almost back to normal, he dressed quickly and angrily picked up the gift he'd been toting around all day, determined to get Tracy Stewart out of his life for good.

11

Tracy stood in the shower letting the water sluice down her back, hoping it would miraculously melt the tension in her shoulders and somehow take away the tightness in her chest. But she knew it would take more than hot water to mend her aching heart. She'd awakened that morning with crusty eyes and a headache, courtesy of a restless night filled with dreams of what should be but couldn't be, and what could be but wouldn't be.

After Susan had dropped her bombshell last night, they'd spoken into the wee hours of the morning. Susan had confided that she and Jeremy had been an item three years ago when he'd come home from his duty overseas to bury his father. The relationship had lasted until he'd shipped out again, but after he'd left there'd been no word from him — no letters, nothing. Even if she'd wanted to contact him, she hadn't a clue as to how to go about it. They'd talked about a lot of things, but his duty overseas wasn't one of them.

Susan had thought their feelings for one another had been mutual, so was already dealing with her broken heart when she realised that, despite having taken precautions, she was pregnant — and with no way to get hold of Jeremy. Susan had eventually decided that if he'd wanted to keep in touch with her, he would have. As far as she had been concerned, Carrie was hers and hers alone. Now that Jeremy was back, she was terrified that if he discovered Carrie was his, he'd try to take her away.

As a lawyer, Tracy knew that was unlikely. Custody arrangements were based on the child's best interests, and since Carrie was only two and had never known her father, her best interest would be to stay in Susan's primary care, although Jeremy would definitely be given access to his child if he wanted it. From what Susan had told her, Jeremy was a decent man who would probably make a good father. Tracy was certain that, between them, they could come up with a joint parenting plan the court would consider.

While this wasn't Tracy's decision to make, she hoped that Susan would do the right thing and tell him about the amazing little girl he'd fathered. He'd missed so much already, he shouldn't miss it all. If Jeremy were the kind, caring, decent man her sister had believed him to be, there was no doubt in Tracy's mind that, once he'd got over the shock and processed all the emotions such news would surely bring, he would honour his newly discovered responsibilities.

Susan was a wonderful mother and Carrie was very lucky to have her, but Tracy couldn't dismiss the importance of having a daddy in a little girl's life — she was and always had been a daddy's girl — and, given the fact that if Jeremy asked for any kind of visitation, the court would include support payments on his part, life would be easier for them too. But despite her personal feelings on the matter, Tracy agreed to keep Susan's secret; she just hoped her sister would reconsider her stand.

When she'd eventually left Susan's room the two of them had never been closer, and although she'd have preferred to have her come back to Eyam, Susan grudgingly accepted Tracy's decision to live in London. They'd hugged, cried, and finally had been able to laugh a little, remembering the good times they'd had growing up. With the air cleared between them, Tracy should have been able to sleep, but her dreams were haunted by visions of a man with dark hair, electric green eyes, and large black-framed glasses.

★　★　★

Tracy turned off the shower, wrapped herself in a fluffy towel, and hurried to get dressed in her cosiest outfit. Her favourite pyjama bottoms had seen better days, as had the ragged old T-shirt that was way too comfortable to throw away. She quickly dried her hair and pulled it back into a ponytail. The image that looked back at her in the mirror didn't resemble a high-powered lawyer in the least. She moisturised her skin and headed downstairs for the next phase of the Stewart Christmas Eve tradition, the reading of *A Christmas Carol*.

As she went down the stairs, Tracy smiled. Despite everything, this had turned out to be the best Christmas Eve ever. It was so true what they said about children creating Christmas spirit. Carrie's enthusiasm had been infectious. The child had been in her element helping to decorate the tree, and the thought of Santa coming and placing all kinds of presents under it later tonight while she slept had her eyes the size of saucers. Everything was new to her, and Tracy got to see the wonder of it all over again. She remembered placing the satin balls on the tree as a child and the way her mother had never moved a single decoration from where she'd placed it. The plastic baubles and elves, rocking horses and angels were all left in Carrie's capable hands, while the more delicate glass ornaments were hung by the adults. When the tree was finished, they all sipped hot chocolate and admired their handiwork.

The house had been filled with music, love, and laughter all day long. There had been no mention of Tracy's absence the last ten years; no mention that she'd be leaving again in just a few short days. It had been wonderful — a family celebrating together, happy to be that way. Every now and then Tracy had noticed Susan watching her daughter with a look of sadness in her eyes. Was she thinking about Jeremy and yet another thing he'd missed in his daughter's life?

The only thing that had persuaded Carrie to take a much-needed nap after lunch had been the promise of biscuit-making when she awoke. Tracy was sure the little girl got more flour and sugar on the floor than she did in the bowl, and despite their best efforts to ensure that she didn't eat any raw dough, Tracy would bet some of it had found its way into her tummy. When it came time to ice the biscuits, Tracy marvelled over each coloured blob, proclaiming them the most beautiful biscuits ever.

With an astonishing number of biscuits eaten and all the excitement of the day, Tracy was amazed to see Carrie dutifully eat all of her tea. Once the meal was over Susan had taken Carrie upstairs for her bath, and Tracy had followed. Despite the offer of help Mum had insisted on cleaning up the kitchen alone, as she always did.

Tracy was the first back downstairs, although she knew Susan wasn't far behind. Earlier in the day a makeshift bed of pillows and blankets had been arranged on the floor where the girls would sit for the traditional reading of Dickens's famous Christmas tale. Tracy had been looking forward to this all day. This had always been her favourite part and she knew that, although the story was a bit complex for a two-year-old, the sound of her father's voice reading the words penned almost two hundred years ago would have the same magical quality for her niece as it had had for her. Susan came into the room with a freshly washed bundle in her arms, a bundle that was holding her favourite toy and blanket, already rubbing her pretty blue eyes.

As her father settled into his comfy chair and her mother sat on the sofa with her knitting in hand, Tracy and Susan, with Carrie between them, curled up on the floor. Dad had barely started chapter one when Tracy heard Carrie's gentle snores. Tracy made sure that she wasn't crowding the child and snuggled into her pillow, listening to her father reading. As she did, she realised how much she'd missed listening to his voice. When she was younger her bedtime ritual had always included Dad sitting on the side of her bed, reading a bedtime story from one of the books that now belonged to Carrie. Through his voice she had discovered the magic of books, and it had inspired her love of reading. Was this another Stewart tradition that would be passed on to Carrie? What of her own children? The ones she hoped to have one day, the ones she'd pictured with dark hair and green eyes? Would they ever get to hear Grandpa read to them like this? She shook off her melancholy and lay lost in the tale, the sweet baby-powder scent of Carrie, and the clicking of her mum's knitting needles.

The moment was almost perfect. Memories of other Christmas Eves when she'd lain like this listening to her dad's voice were slowly replaced by memories of another man's voice reading to her — his passionate kisses, his unmistakable fear for her when he'd gallantly rescued her, and the confused, angry, hurt look on his face when she'd driven away from him last night.

'Tracy,' her mum called, snapping her out of her reverie. 'Tracy, you have a visitor.' From the sound of her voice, it was someone her mother was pleased to see. Who would be here to see her tonight of all nights?

'Come on in, Mike,' her mother said in her most welcoming tone. 'We're all in the living room listening to Henry read *A Christmas Carol*; it's a family tradition.'

Mike! Tracy jumped up abruptly. Panic suffused her and the sudden movement disturbed Carrie, who began to fuss. Tracy froze, afraid to move again until Carrie settled. Susan rubbed her daughter's back and cooed softly to her.

'Thanks, Mrs. Stewart, but I can't stop. I just needed to speak to Tracy for a minute.'

'She'll be right here. I can't imagine

what's keeping her. Tracy, you have company.'

'Coming, Mum,' she called, horrified at the prospect that Mike was about to see her in the most unflattering clothes she owned. They might be comfy, but they were a far cry from the lingerie most men seemed to expect women to wear. She was about to pull out the pony tail, but without a brush she'd look even worse with her hair wild about her face.

And why bother? He was probably just there to reiterate that he never wanted to see her again. The idea made her heart sink. Deep down she'd hoped that things were fixable between them, especially now that she understood Susan's flight. She couldn't tell Mike the whole truth, but she could definitely admit Susan and Jeremy had a history — one that Susan didn't care to revisit.

She sighed, wishing to avoid a confrontation, but since he was here and his mother had seen him, there was no way she could just brush him off.

She took a deep breath, lifted her chin and walked out of the living room into the hall.

'Hi.' She was annoyed by the breathless sound of her voice.

'Hi yourself,' he replied, emotionless.

Tracy's mother disappeared, tactfully closing the door to the sitting room behind her. Tracy indicated the chair in the hallway before sitting down on the bottom step of the stairs, but Mike remained standing. She was glad of the closed door — she didn't want her family to hear Mike telling her off again.

'What are you doing here? I thought you were finished with me.' She wrapped her arms around herself, more for comfort than out of defiance. The man had broken her heart. As she stared into his breathtakingly beautiful green eyes, she thought she saw a flash of sadness at her words.

Mike ran his hand through his hair in his signature move. She noticed that his other hand was behind his back and was surprised when he pulled it out and extended it towards her. It contained a box wrapped in Christmas paper, a print of Santa Clauses riding motorcycles. It was adorable, and her eyes brimmed with tears.

'I brought you a Christmas present. It's of no use to me, so you might as well have it.' He thrust the package at her, and she had no choice but to accept it.

'What is it?' she asked, confused by his actions. She didn't know whether to be happy with the fact that he'd bought her a gift, or upset by the finality of his words. She felt a little guilty since she'd not thought to get him anything. She had planned to pick up something today, but their confrontation last night had changed her mind.

'Open it,' he said, and she sensed anxiety behind his request.

Tracy smiled as she carefully opened the package. There were two kinds of gift-openers — savers and rippers. Susan was a ripper, tearing at the paper to get to the prize beneath, but Tracy had always been a saver, carefully lifting each piece of tape to ensure that the paper wasn't damaged. She did the same this time, slowly unwrapping the gift, not wanting to tear a single Santa. When the gift was fully exposed, she frowned. These were the books she'd purchased on her first day home. Confused, she looked up at him.

'Look inside the front cover,' he instructed.

She did as she was told. Inside the book, on the face page, she saw her gift:

'For Tracy, the woman I hope will always be my greatest fan. G.L. O'Michael.'

She squealed and launched herself into Mike's arms, raining kisses on his face.

'Thank you so much! I love them!' she said and was about to kiss him properly when she realised how rigidly he held himself, his arms hanging at his sides. She reluctantly backed away from him.

She sat back down, the books in her lap, trying to regain some of her dignity. She took a couple of deep breaths in an effort to calm herself and wondered vaguely why he was still here. She loved her gift and didn't want to seem ungrateful, but since they had nothing more to say to one another, she was at a loss.

'How did you manage to get these so quickly?' She hoped it hadn't been too much trouble, considering the way things had gone south between them.

Mike stood silently looking down at her, running his hand through his hair, clearly struggling with something. She hoped that something was changing his mind about them, so she could kiss him the way she desperately wanted to; but she could see that whatever it was, the struggle was tearing him apart and the concern on his face was painful to see.

He'd been absolutely right last night. She had been putting up roadblocks in their relationship, and he deserved to be happy. He deserved someone who didn't come with as much emotional baggage as she did, someone who'd be content to make Eyam home. She wanted to share her hopes and fears with him. She knew she was selfish and had issues when it came to trust and control, but she desperately wanted Mike to be the man she allowed into her life.

She thought of the day she'd had, reliving the Stewart Christmas traditions though Carrie's eyes, and she knew she wanted that for her children too. The fact that he was still here had to mean something. Maybe there was still a chance, but unless she was honest about things, it was a slim one at best. She needed to tell him how she felt about him. She had to take a leap of faith that he wouldn't throw her love back in her face. Was he really done with her? She had to know for sure, and if the price was further heartbreak, then so be it.

'Mike . . . ' she began, but he cut her off.

'Tracy, I am G.L. O'Michael. It's my pen name.' The words rushed out of his mouth.

Tracy stared at him. He had to be joking. There was no way he could have stood there in the bookshop a few days ago, listening to her gush and go on and on about how much she loved the books, if he'd been the author. He wouldn't have played her for a fool like that. He'd refused to betray his friend and had even played along when she'd made her vow to discover the truth. He couldn't be that devious.

'That's not funny, Mike.' She set the books to one side and looked at him.

'It's the truth, Tracy. I know what I said last night, and I meant it then, but being here with you now, all I want to do is unsay what I said and find a way to make things work between us. I can't do that and keep this secret.' She could hear the sincerity in his words, and her heart blocked her throat. It couldn't be true.

'I don't believe you,' she whispered,

hoping against hope that he was lying, and that this was all some kind of hoax. She loved this man, wanted to trust him; but if he'd been toying with her, making her feel like the world's biggest fool, there was no chance for them, no chance at all.

He shook his head. 'I'm sorry for keeping this from you, Tracy. G is for Gareth, my middle name. L is for Lawrence, my grandfather's name. O'Michael is . . . well, self-explanatory. I'm telling you the truth.'

Listening to his explanation, she realised it made perfect sense. Hadn't she supposed that the author might have used the name O'Michael in a nod to his friend? Suddenly all the pieces fell into place — of course the author would have advance copies. How could she have not seen it? How could she have been so clueless? So stupid? Anger at being played for a fool surged through her.

'So this whole time you've been lying to me?' What was left of Tracy's heart shattered; she couldn't even look at him.

'Not exactly lying, Tracy. As a lawyer, you know people tell half-truths all the time. I do know G.L. O'Michael; we did go to school together; I just didn't tell you that he's part of me — my alter ego. G.L. O'Michael has a much more exciting life than Mike O'Neill ever did — until I met you. I'm sorry for not telling you sooner, but the only other people who know the truth are my immediate family and my publisher. Now you do, too. It isn't something I want spread around the village. I value my privacy.'

'Don't worry, Mike. Your secret is safe with me. Will you please leave now?'

'Please, Tracy, I want this to work between us . . .'

'Leave! Go now!' She spat the words at him, her face a mask of fury. No one made a fool of her — not anymore. She sat on the stairs looking down until she heard the front door close and the sound of his bike start, the crush of gravel beneath his wheels and the gradual fade as he disappeared down the road. Once he was gone, she crumbled, her tears flowing freely.

12

Mike rode away from Tracy for the first and probably the last time. He'd blown it! He'd intended to go there, give her the gift, and leave, hoping it would put an end to his dreams of a future with her. When he'd seen her, in pyjamas that had seen better days, her face fresh and clear of make-up, her hair pulled back from her face giving her an innocence that belied her life experiences, he'd been lost. She'd looked so tiny, so fragile, trying to act tough, and all he'd wanted to do was sweep her up and carry her away somewhere so he could show her exactly how he felt about her.

The only thing stopping him from doing just that had been the secret he'd been keeping from her. He'd given her the books and told her the truth, but her reaction hadn't been what he'd expected. He'd thought she might be annoyed with him for not being honest and up-front with her, but he hadn't anticipated the pain and the anger. He'd assumed discovering that the man she was seeing was her favourite author would be exciting for her. She'd certainly been thrilled when she'd seen the autographed dedications.

His feigned indifference when she'd thrown herself at him in gratitude had been his second mistake. He should have responded to her kisses the way he wanted to. Delivering his news after they'd made up properly would have been a better idea. Instead, he'd climbed up on his soap box and confessed his sins. He'd gone about it in completely the wrong way, and now he didn't know how to fix things.

Surely she should have been happy? But the voice of reason at the back of his mind told him he had to be kidding. He'd been lying to her; had even made a joke about it — all of it at her expense, so he could spend time with her. No doubt she'd felt used and humiliated. Not exactly an auspicious way to start a relationship. There'd been mutual interest there, but would she have given him the time of day without his G.L. O'Michael ploy? He'd never know. If she'd been interested before, she was definitely not interested now.

Mike continued berating himself for his stupidity as he travelled swiftly towards home. It was darker tonight since there was only a quarter-moon to add light to the sky full of stars, but the gloominess seemed to fit his mood. The streets were deserted; since he wasn't focusing on his riding, that was probably a good thing. He was almost home when he noticed something strange — a steady stream of smoke flooding the sky, coming from a point somewhere in the heart of the village. His instinct told him something was very wrong and, making a split-second decision, he veered away from his homeward route, instead heading towards what his gut told him was some kind of fire. It had to be. And on Christmas Eve! All he could do was hope that if it was a house fire, everyone was out safely. No one should die tonight.

Rounding the corner of the High Street, his heart sank as he saw that his hunch had been right — smoke was coming from the back of old Mrs. Townley's house. Screeching to a halt outside the front lawn, he grabbed his mobile and called 999. At the noise from his engine, neighbours from several of the surrounding houses looked out of their windows and took in the scene before them. Shocked faces disappeared from windows and reappeared at their front doors, as did, thankfully, old Mrs. Townley, who stumbled out of her house, looking equal parts dazed and horrified as she tried to make sense of what was happening around her.

Mike went to the shocked woman and draped his leather jacket over her shoulders, shouting for someone to bring a chair and a blanket. Moments later a dining room chair had appeared, and he eased Mrs. Townley into it and wrapped her shivering frame in the thick blanket which another helpful neighbour had quickly supplied. Mike bent down to speak to Mrs. Townley, who sat silently weeping.

'I'm so sorry about your house. The fire services will be here soon and they'll do all they can to save it — but you're safe, and that's what matters.'

'Peaches is still inside,' wailed Mrs. Townley.

The news struck Mike harder than it probably should have, but he'd lost so much tonight, he didn't want to see anyone lose anything else. That ginger tabby was all the family the octogenarian had left.

Mike looked at the burning building. The fire looked to still be contained to the back, but with the fire engines nowhere in sight just yet, who knew how long it would be — and how much the fire would have progressed — before Peaches was in with a chance of rescue? Mike knew that what he was considering was both foolish and dangerous, but he had to do something.

'Where was Peaches, Mrs. Townley, before you got out?'

'She usually sleeps in the kitchen.' Tears flowed down her smoke-smudged cheeks.

The kitchen was to the side of the house, at the front. Reckless as it was, Mike decided to give it a shot. He headed to the front door and entered the burning building.

Other than being filled with smoke, the front part of the house seemed unaffected, but Mike knew that could be deceptive. He hurried to the kitchen door, which was firmly shut, and opened it — to be almost barrelled over by a streak of ginger fur. Peaches shot through the door and straight up onto Mike's chest, digging his claws in painfully. With the cat held securely in his arms, Mike turned tail himself and ran for the front door, not wanting to spend a second longer than he had to in the way of danger.

He handed a slightly-the-worse-for-wear Peaches to Mrs. Townley, who couldn't stop crying her thanks, just as a fire engine roared to a stop in front of the old house, closely followed by an ambulance. A paramedic came over and tried to attend to the old lady, who adamantly refused to let go of the cat. Mike turned to give the paramedic some space to work and was almost barrelled over for the second time in as many minutes by a small body raining blows on his chest — which was still smarting from Peaches' assault — while crying and screaming at him.

'Whoa! Whoa!' yelled Mike. He reached out to grab the person who was using him as a punching bag and his heart almost stopped when he realised it was Tracy pummelling him. Tears streamed down her face as she continued to cry and yell incoherently at him. She was still dressed in her old pyjamas, but her hair had come loose and fell in waves around her face. Her eyes were puffy and swollen, her face red and blotchy, and she was blubbering all kinds of nonsense. She'd never looked more beautiful.

'Tracy, calm down. What's the matter?'

'What's the matter?' she shrieked. 'You're the matter! You could have been killed, you great idiot!' She pulled away from him, her hands fisted at her side, shaking in her fury. She reminded him of an enraged cartoon character, and if she hadn't looked so terrified he might have laughed; but unwilling to risk her wrath again, he thought better of it.

'You stupid, stupid, stupid man!' she spat at him, pounding him in the chest to emphasise her words.

'Tracy, I'm fine. You don't need to worry about me.' He reached to grab her hands to stop the abuse, but she backed away out of reach.

She crossed her arms around herself. 'What you did was stupid and reckless.

I couldn't have managed if you'd died. Did you think of that when you went into that house? Did you think of anyone else?'

Where had this come from? She'd made it pretty clear that their relationship was over. Did he dare hope differently?

'What do you mean you couldn't have managed?'

'I love you, you idiot!' she shouted, loud enough for the entire village to hear.

Mike gawked at her. He looked stunned.

Tracy stared at him and tried to hold on to her rage, but the adrenaline surge that had driven her to blurt out her feelings like that was waning. The emotional turmoil of the evening had taken its toll. She looked at Mike, waiting for some kind of a reaction to her hastily shouted declaration of love, but he just stood there, mouth agape, staring at her.

How dare he endanger himself like

that? His face was soot-smudged, his beautiful emerald eyes wide and staring. Unease crept into her. She knew she'd surprised him, probably more than she'd expected, but the longer he stood there gasping like a fish out of water the more uncomfortable she felt. She'd just confessed her love for him in a very public way and he seemed flummoxed, looking at her as if she'd arrived from a different planet and saying nothing. Not exactly the reaction she might have hoped for. She'd thought he might have cared for her after what he'd said. She must have been wrong.

An hour ago she'd still been sitting at home hugging the books to her and crying into Susan's shoulder, wondering how things could have gone so wrong. He shouldn't have kept his secret from her, but the more she thought about it the more she realised that it was exactly what she would have done had the situation been reversed.

She knew G.L. O'Michael valued his

anonymity, so why was she surprised he hadn't been willing to share his identity with a virtual stranger? It wasn't as if she'd given him many opportunities to come clean about it either. In fact, being with Mike had all but driven G.L. O'Michael out of her mind.

Although Susan kept asking what they'd argued about, Tracy had refused to answer, simply saying it was stupid and not worth discussing. Susan hadn't pried, and she was grateful for that. She had just stopped crying when the phone rang. Moments later her mother had come into the room, all worry, and insisted that Tracy and Susan come with her to check on Mrs. Townley, whose house was on fire. She hadn't even given them time to change; they'd just thrown coats on over their pyjamas and headed out.

When they'd arrived at the scene the house was in flames, and Tracy's heart had stopped when Mrs. Townley had said that Mike was inside looking for Peaches. She looked at the blazing structure and knew without a doubt that life wouldn't be worth living without him — she loved him. Yes it had only been four days, but her heart knew and recognised its soulmate even if her brain didn't.

Tracy promised herself that as soon as she saw Mike, she'd tell him that she loved him. No more holding back, no more selfishly guarding her heart. She was all in — her heart belonged to Mike.

When Mike continued to remain silent, she was certain that he was going to take her declaration of love and discard it, and what little rage and fear that remained began to change into sorrow.

He didn't feel the same way.

She'd made a deal with herself, so she followed through on her promise to herself. Mike was safe; that was all that really mattered. She couldn't stay here looking at the man who was crushing her heart piece by piece. She turned away from him, prepared to walk away with whatever shreds of her dignity remained before she gave way to tears and crumbled to the ground in anguish, when he gently took her arm, preventing her from leaving.

He pulled her towards him, his face deadly serious as he looked down at her. He took her face in his hands and bent down so that he could look her in the eyes.

'I love you too, Tracy. I'm sorry I upset you. In fact, I'm sorry about everything that happened tonight. I was wrong to keep that secret from you, and I didn't really think about just how risky it was to go in after Peaches.' His words made her heart soar.

She stood on tiptoes, meeting him halfway, and poured every ounce of her love into the kiss she gave him. Suddenly she realised she needed him in the same way she needed air to breathe. How was she ever going to be able to leave this man? She forgot where she was and the crowds around them. All that mattered was Mike.

When he lifted her into his arms she wrapped her legs around his waist and continued to kiss him.

Somehow they had to find a way to make this work — she wanted this man in her life. In fact, she couldn't imagine life without him. There were no more secrets. Everything was out in the open. Surely they could be together? Mike slowly pulled his mouth away and lowered her feet to the ground, his breathing as ragged as hers.

'Sorry to intrude, but I just wanted to say thank you before they take me to the hospital.' Mrs. Townley smiled. 'You're a very brave man, Mike.'

Tracy stood wrapped in Mike's arms, dazed from his kisses, and the knowledge that her life had changed irrevocably. She watched the old lady stroke the purring cat.

Mike smiled down at the grateful woman. 'Don't mention it, Mrs. Townley. I'm glad I was able to save Peaches, and I'd gladly do it again just to find out this woman loves me and hear her say those wonderful words.'

'Oh, how sweet.' She waved as the paramedics whisked her away.

Mike looked down at Tracy, who screwed up her face to look as cross as she possibly could. 'Over my dead body,' she warned him. 'No more putting yourself in danger like that. But I do love you, you big idiot!' She lifted her face up to him, inviting another kiss. She'd never get enough of this delicious man.

'Michael Gareth O'Neill, as I live and breathe, if you ever do anything as stupid as that again, I will turn you over my knee, and don't you think you're too big for me to do it!' yelled Brenda, rushing up to her son and causing Tracy to jump away as if she'd been burned. But Mike wouldn't let her go.

13

Tracy looked around, suddenly aware of where they were and the people surrounding them, and she felt the heat rise in her face. Somewhere in the crowd Susan and her mother had been witnesses to her declaration of love, as had most of the village. She and Mike had certainly given the gossip mill enough fuel to keep it running for days, but for the first time in her life she didn't care. Let them talk.

Mike's mother hadn't stopped berating her son. 'When Mrs. Harper called me and told me you'd gone into that house after Peaches, I almost had a heart attack! What were you thinking, risking your life like that?'

Mr. O'Neill reached his wife and extended a hand to pat his son on the back. Tracy saw the gleam of pride and respect on the older man's face, so similar to the one she loved. 'You did give us a scare, but that was a great thing you did; that cat means the world to Mrs. Townley. Just don't do it again.'

Mike looked over at his parents, a sheepish smile on his face. 'Tracy's already given me a ticking-off about it. I wasn't thinking — but I'm safe, Peaches is safe, and that's really all that matters. Nobody deserves to lose someone they love on Christmas Eve.'

The scowl on his mother's face gradually eased and turned into a smile as she looked at Tracy, still in Mike's arms. 'I'm glad to see you two have patched up your differences. That's good. But it won't stop me from getting on at you if you even think of doing something like this again. Now, are we heading home?'

Tracy pivoted with Mike as they turned to look at the house. The structure was still in flames, but the firefighters manning the hoses were pouring water onto the fire and it was more or less contained.

'Not just yet, Mum,' Mike said. 'I have a feeling I'm going to need to stay here and give statements or something. Plus, I just feel like I should be here in case there's anything I can do to help.' Turning to Tracy, he said, 'I love you,' before walking off in the direction of the fire engine.

'Are you going to come back to the house with us?' asked Brenda, turning to Tracy. 'He probably won't be more than an hour or so. I know he'd be glad to see you when he gets home, and something tells me you two have unfinished business.'

Tracy blushed clear through to the roots of her hair. As much as she'd love to see Mike later on, knowing that he was okay and that everything was going to work out between them, it was Christmas Eve and she needed to get back home and get some sleep. She didn't want to risk missing seeing Carrie's face first thing in the morning for anything.

'Thanks, Brenda, but I have to go

home. I'll talk to Mike tomorrow.'

She turned to look back at her man, the hero. Smiling contentedly, she turned and almost ran straight into her mum. Tracy cringed, fearing she was in for a tongue-lashing about the spectacle she'd made of herself in front of the village.

'Evening, Brenda. That son of yours is quite the hero. Mrs. Townley can't say enough about him. You must be very proud.' She turned to Tracy, seeming to study her. 'So you're in love, I see.'

'Yes, I am,' Tracy replied, surprised by her mum's tone. It wasn't at all what she'd been expecting.

A smile spread across her mum's face, and she took Tracy in her arms and gave her a hug. The public display of emotion on her mother's part surprised her, but Tracy readily accepted the sign of approbation and love.

'That's great. I'm happy for you. Mike is a really good man.'

'Yes, he is.'

They said goodbye to the O'Neills, and her mother led her over to the car where Susan was waiting. Tracy looked back again at Mike. She certainly had a lot to be grateful for this Christmas Eve.

★　★　★

Tracy sat at the kitchen table drinking the cup of chamomile tea her mother had insisted she have in an effort to calm herself after the emotional rollercoaster their evening had been, but the soothing brew had no effect on her taut nerves. She was way too excited. For the first time in forever, everything was right with her world.

Yes, there were things that she and Mike would have to work out to make the long-distance relationship work, but others had done it. She loved him and he loved her. His words echoed in her head for what seemed like the hundredth time. She was certain if she went outside now, her glowing smile would be visible from space. She pushed the brew away, stood, picked up the cup, and walked over to empty it in the sink. Her mobile phone rang. She picked it up quickly, and smiled when she saw who it was.

'Hey, gorgeous.' Her heart skipped a beat at the sound of Mike's voice.

'Hi,' she answered shyly, as she turned out the light in the kitchen and headed up the stairs. The house was comfortably quiet. Santa had done his job and a mountain of gifts waited under the tree. It was almost one and Carrie would be up by six.

'I'd like to say I'm sorry I scared you tonight, but considering how things turned out I wouldn't really mean it, and the last thing I ever want to do is lie to you again.'

She laughed and closed the door to her room, lying on the bed to continue the conversation. 'Fine — just no more cat-rescuing, especially not from burning buildings.'

She heard him chortle. 'Yes, miss. Between you and my mother, if I do, my life won't be worth living. Speaking of tomorrow — or rather today now — I know it's Christmas Day today, but since you did tell me you loved me, I was hoping that meant I warranted some time with you. I don't want to intrude on your family's Christmas, but maybe just a quick visit?'

'Hmm . . . I did tell you I loved you, didn't I? Well, I suppose I could spare some time for the man I love.' She heard Mike laugh on the other end of the line. His laughter was like a song she could listen to over and over again, just enjoying the sound of it.

'I don't think I'll ever get tired of hearing you say those words. And if it's okay with you, there's somewhere I'd really like to take you — maybe on Boxing Day?'

Tracy got butterflies in her stomach, a combination of excitement and anxiety.

'Back to the Peaks, or do you have

some other private yet potentially dangerous spot in mind?' she asked hesitantly.

'No, and this is someplace it's unlikely you'll venture off to on your own and get lost in. It's beautiful and private, and I promise to keep you safe from any potential danger — I won't let anything happen to the woman I love,' he said with a smile in his voice.

'Well, any time after two o'clock tomorrow is fine. We have Christmas dinner early. After that, we just sit around and relax. I'll have to check with Mum about Boxing Day though — it's been so long since I've spent Christmas here, I feel I should spend as much time as possible with my family while I'm still here.'

Mike understood. 'Okay then, see you very soon. Merry Christmas, Tracy. I love you. Sweet dreams.'

'Merry Christmas, Mike. I love you too. Get some rest.' She ended the call before he heard the squeal that threatened to escape her lips. She turned into her pillow, allowing it to escape, muffled by the pillow. She felt like a teenager, head over heels in love, an emotion she'd never experienced back then. It felt wonderful.

★   ★   ★

Christmas morning came early, and Tracy spent much of it playing princesses and having tea parties with Carrie, although it seemed the child spent as much time playing with the boxes her gifts had come in as she did with the gifts themselves. With the exception of the tea set Tracy had bought her, the stuffed pink unicorn, and the princess dress-up clothes, she liked the boxes best. Tracy laughed as she watched the child climb into the largest one and hide herself inside along with the unicorn. Susan stood poised to catch her if the box tipped over.

The morning had passed quickly, and Christmas dinner had been superb, as always. The dinner conversation had ranged from the wonderful Christmas Eve they'd spent together to Mike's daring rescue of Peaches. Her father was looking forward to shaking Mike's hand later on that afternoon, and Tracy had blushed every shade of red imaginable as Susan had described the touching love scene she'd witnessed between Tracy and Mike, adding in all kinds of dramatic pauses and sound effects that had everyone laughing, including Tracy herself. She was sure that a short, angry woman in worn-out pyjamas beating up a cat-rescuing hero must have looked every bit as funny as it sounded.

She'd been surprised and relieved when her parents had been absolutely fine about Mike's plans to whisk her off on Boxing Day. The wistful look on Susan's face had almost broken her heart though. Tracy felt guilty. Her sister was clearly unhappy, and there was nothing she could do to change that.

As her mum had started to clear the

dinner things away, Tracy had excused herself and gone upstairs to freshen up before Mike's arrival. She'd just finished brushing her hair when Susan came into her room.

'I'm so happy for you,' Susan said to her sister.

'Thank you. I wish I could help you find some happiness, or even just some peace.'

Susan looked on the verge of tears. Tracy decided she might as well be upfront with Susan about her thoughts on what she knew was tormenting Susan.

'Just a phone call, Susan. Just tell him, and let the cards fall where they may. I promise you, Carrie won't be taken away from you, from us — but she might just gain a father, and how wonderful would that be for her?'

Susan nodded, the tears finally spilling over.

'Maybe you're right,' she said quietly.

The sisters hugged, then walked downstairs and started to tidy up the mess Carrie had made. The child's voice could be heard coming from the large box she'd chosen as her special place. Tracy knew Susan would soon cart the little girl upstairs for her nap.

As Tracy folded the sheets of wrapping paper Carrie had been playing with, the butterflies in her stomach moved to full alert. Mike would be here in less than fifteen minutes. She'd taken care with her appearance, wearing her tight black skinny jeans and a lacy red Christmas sweater. She'd used make-up sparingly and had added eye shadow and mascara.

Last night she'd been running on adrenaline, and although she'd relived the words they'd shared a hundred times, she hadn't been able to come to grips with the implications of them. There was no doubt in her mind that she loved Mike, and he'd said he felt the same way, but what role had last night's circumstances played in their declarations? He'd been as high on adrenaline as she'd been — hers from fear, his from exhilaration. Did he still feel the same way now? He'd said he loved her when he'd called in the wee hours, and again this morning when he'd call to firm up the plans. She'd heard his parents shouting 'Merry Christmas' in the background, and it didn't sound as if anything had changed. Brenda had even insisted that she come over for a visit, maybe tomorrow afternoon when they got back, so he'd obviously told them his plans. He'd ended the conversation by telling her he loved her.

She knew she didn't have a lot of experience with relationships, but why was she suddenly so unsure of herself? Taking a deep breath, she decided she was driving herself crazy for nothing and jumped when she heard the sound of Mike's bike pulling into the drive-way.

Turning to her family, she asked quickly, for what must have been the tenth time, 'Now, before he comes in, are you all absolutely sure it's okay for me to see Mike tomorrow?'

'Yes!' her father, mother and sister spoke in unison.

Tracy was touched. She hadn't expected this level of love and support. They'd told her over and over again how pleased they were for her and Mike, and what a great couple they made. Her mother was adamant that if Tracy were following her heart, as she believed she was, everything would work out.

'It's never steered you wrong before,' she added solemnly. Tracy wasn't sure when the relationship she'd had with her mum had changed, but suddenly they were comfortable together, and she wouldn't change that for the world.

'Merry Christmas, everyone.' Mike stepped through the open doorway and kissed Tracy on the cheek. 'I have a present for Carrie.'

'Present?' squealed a little voice coming from a large box in the middle of the living room. He spotted dark blonde curls barely visible at the top of the box. He smiled at the sight and walked over to the box to give her the gift. Lesley's boys had been the same at that age, and they still hadn't outgrown their love of a good box. At their age, it could become almost anything, and his sister's children had vivid imaginations.

He handed the brightly wrapped present into the box and a second later, it tipped over to reveal Carrie clutching the Dora sound and storybook he'd brought her.

'Look, Mum. Read it, please?' She thrust the book toward her mother.

'Of course, sweetheart, but what do we say to Uncle Mike?'

Carrie looked at him shyly, just as her gorgeous aunt had earlier. 'Thank you, Uncle Mike.'

'You're welcome.' She was such a sweetheart. He wondered if he and Tracy had a little girl, would she look like this little angel?

He felt arms he recognised wrap themselves around his waist.

'That was really thoughtful of you,' Tracy said, and kissed his cheek.

* * *

The rest of the day settled into a warm, comfortable and quietly joyful one — the perfect family Christmas. After Carrie had gone to bed the adults sat in the living room bathed in the soft glow of the Christmas tree lights, chatting and reminiscing, picking at chocolates and drinking endless cups of tea. As the evening drew in and yawns replaced chatter, first her mum and dad and then Susan excused themselves, wished Mike a Merry Christmas once more, and went to bed — something Tracy couldn't help feeling was partly for her benefit!

Now they were by themselves, Mike turned to her and said, 'I have something for you, too.'

'But you already gave me my gift — Mr. O'Michael!' teased Tracy.

He reached into his jacket for a small

box and handed it to her. Tracy took the box and slowly opened it. Inside was a beautiful silver, aquamarine and turquoise ring.

'Oh, Mike! It's beautiful.'

'I wanted you to have a permanent reminder of how much I love you. You mean the world to me, Tracy. I want us to be together — I think you do too.' She was about to speak, but he put his finger on her mouth to stop her.

'Don't say anything; just think about what I said. I love you. Eyam is where I belong, but we have to find some way to make this work because not being with you isn't a viable alternative.'

Mike didn't know what would happen when it was time for Tracy to return to the city, but they had another week together before they needed to think about that. They were both here now, and he was going to enjoy every minute of their time together. They could deal with the hard stuff later. He bent his head, kissed her deeply, and then slowly, reluctantly, moved away from her. 'It's late. I should really get back home. But I'll see you tomorrow. Merry Christmas, Tracy.'

'Merry Christmas, Mike. Thank you.' She kissed him once more and went with him to the front door. He walked to his bike, got on, and rode off towards home.

Tracy stared at the ring and thought of what it represented. What would it cost her to say she'd stay in Eyam and build a life with the man she loved? The answer was clear — her hopes, her dreams, her career, and her life in London. Was the price steeper than she was willing to pay?

14

Tracy awoke rested and surprised she'd slept at all. She climbed out of bed and into the shower, and as the water sluiced over her she thought of what Mike had said. He loved her; he wanted to make it work. She did too, didn't she? But he'd hated the city, and her time in Eyam was coming to an end; she'd have to return to London. She didn't know how she was going to leave him. She turned off the shower and reached for her towel.

She'd just finished drying her hair when her mobile phone rang, and assuming it was Mike, she answered without checking who the caller was.

'Hi, handsome.'

The laughter at the end of the line startled her.

'You've called me a lot of things over the years, Tracy,' said Mark, one of the paralegals she worked with in London, 'but handsome isn't one of them. I'm not sure my partner would be happy if you started. I gather you've enjoyed your holiday?'

'Hi, Mark.' She tried to sound friendly, but she couldn't keep the dread out of her voice. If he was calling her here, any news he had to give her wouldn't be good. 'I'm enjoying it. I still have a week left.'

'Sorry, Trace; you don't. The boss wants you here by noon tomorrow, or someone else is getting that junior partnership you've got your heart set on, and you'll probably be looking for a new job. He's sending his newest junior partner — that would be you — to New York in two days' time. I get to go as your underling and we need to be there a.s.a.p. We can count on being there for the foreseeable future, by the looks of things. How soon can you get back here and pack for the Big Apple?'

She stared at the phone, as if by doing so she could make it vanish. No.

This couldn't be happening. She couldn't leave now, not like this. New York? America? She might as well be moving to the moon. Promotion or not, leaving now was the last thing she wanted to do.

'Tracy, are you still there?'

'Sorry Mark, I have to call you back.' She ended the call and threw herself down on the bed, tears of sorrow and disappointment soaking her pillow in no time.

When she managed to control herself, she went downstairs, grateful the only one in the kitchen was her father. Unfortunately, despite the artfully applied make-up, he could read her like a book.

'Oh love, what's wrong?' The look of concern on his face forced her tears to the surface once more.

'Everything! I have to go back to London tomorrow, and I'm getting that junior partnership and being sent out to our U.S. offices for goodness knows how long.'

'Isn't this what you've always wanted? Maybe not going to America, but the partnership?'

'Yes.' She hiccupped, and the tears continued to roll down her cheeks.

'Why do I get the feeling that it might not be what you want anymore?'

'I don't know; I don't know what I want. When I came home, I was going to spend the holidays here, and then go back to London and work until I earned that promotion. Now that it's mine, it doesn't seem so attractive anymore. And there's Mike.'

Her father shook his head. 'Tracy, years ago I told you to follow your heart. It's never let you down. Whatever you decide to do, your mum and I and Susan will support you. I'll wager Mike will do whatever he can for you too, because all a good man wants to do is make the woman he loves happy.' He poured her a cup of coffee. 'Listen to your heart.'

Tracy put her arms around him. 'How come you're so wise?' she sniffed.

247

He smiled. 'I've spent almost forty years trying to make your mother happy. She's my world. I can recognise a man and woman in love when I see them. I had a bit of a scare last autumn — don't look at me like that — my cholesterol was high, and I needed to lose some weight. I even had to give up those cigars of mine, but I'd do anything to keep your mum from worrying. Sometimes you have to do what's best, even if you don't want to do it. But you always have to be true to yourself, and follow your heart.'

Her mobile phone rang and it was Mike. She took a deep breath, still not sure what she was going to tell him.

'Morning, gorgeous.' She could hear the warmth and love in his voice. 'Are you ready for our Boxing Day trip?

'Yes, I am.' She realised that the sound of his voice had made the decision for her. 'When will you pick me up?'

'The sooner the better. Say, two hours?'

'I'll be waiting.' She had a lot to do between now and then. She hung up the phone.

* * *

Two hours later, when Mike pulled up in front of Tracy's home, he could tell she was giddy with excitement. She looked happy and well-rested. He wished he could say the same. He'd hardly slept all night. Instead of the dreams he'd anticipated, he'd been plagued with nightmares of Tracy telling him she was leaving him and Eyam and never coming back. The news his mother had given him this morning hadn't made him feel any better.

As she came towards him, he got off his bike and met her halfway. He pulled her into his arms and captured her mouth, all his need and frustration evident in the kiss.

'I missed you.' He held her close a moment longer before releasing her.

She had a mischievous look in her eye. 'I missed you too.'

He took a deep breath and plunged in with the news that had been troubling him all morning.

'Your mum called mine early this morning and said you got the summons from London. When do you have to go back?' He didn't want to hear her answer, terrified that his nightmare was about to come true. If she left him now, he didn't know how he'd manage. He'd decided that if London was where she needed to be, then he'd move there. If he had to, G.L. O'Michael could write anywhere; perhaps if they found a house just outside the city, it would work for both of them. They could come back to Eyam for holidays. It wasn't a perfect solution, but he'd do what it took to make the woman he loved happy. It was all about being together. Where that happened to be didn't make much difference.

Tracy nestled into him. 'One of my colleagues called with news from the boss, so I've had a chat with him and I'll probably go back next week or the week after. There's no rush, really.'

Mike was confused. 'The week after next? Have you extended your holiday? What did your boss have to say?'

'I've been offered that junior partnership I wanted. I just have to work from our U.S. offices in New York for a few months, a couple of years at the most.'

Mike's breath caught in his throat. New York! How could she stand there and tell him she was moving to New York? He was ready to panic, but forced his emotions down. New York was just another city, after all.

'It's what you've always wanted, isn't it? You mentioned it's what you'd been working towards. A junior partnership in a prestigious international firm has always been your dream.'

'True.' She snuggled closer into his body, but Mike couldn't enjoy the feeling of having her close. His whole future, their life together, hung in the balance.

'I know I said that moving to the city would be too hard for me, but I've been rethinking that. I can't let you go. We belong together. I'll find a way to make it work — maybe we can get a place just outside of London, or New York, or wherever you choose to be.' He waited for her reaction, surprised when she didn't say anything. 'Tracy, did you hear what I said? I'll leave Eyam. I'll go with you. When do we have to leave?'

'Mike, that you'd do that for me is the sweetest, most wonderful thing I've ever heard, but I couldn't ask you to do it. You'd be miserable, and I'd be miserable seeing you that way. There's no rush. I can go and get my stuff any time I want.'

'Tracy, you're not making sense.'

'Did I mention I gave him my decision already?'

She was killing him. 'For God's sake, don't torture me this way. What decision did you make?'

She smiled up at him, her beautiful

face glowing. Her eyes shone. 'I handed in my notice. There was no way I could leave the man I love to go to New York for goodness knows how long.'

Mike held her close against him, all the fear and relief he'd felt mixing together. When he was sure she understood how much losing her would have meant to him, he released her.

'So what are you going to do? Look for another job in London? With your track record, that should be a snap.'

She smiled impishly. 'I do have to go back to London to empty my flat and get the rest of my things. I have a few cases to wrap up and hand over before I start my new job.'

'You've got a new job already?' He felt his hopes plummet, but tried to rally his emotions. So what if she was going back to London — at least they would still be in the same country as each other!

'I have. The hours are great, and I'll have lots of free time. I told you about Mr. White's offer, remember? Well, I took him up on it. You did say you wanted me to stay, didn't you?' She smiled cheekily at him as his mouth dropped open.

'You little minx. You enjoyed watching me suffer thinking you were leaving, didn't you?

'Maybe just a little bit — call it payback for not telling me the truth about yourself.'

He threw back his head and laughed, full of joy. 'I can't tell you how happy being on the receiving end of that payback has just made me!'

They grinned at each other, the future starting to take shape before them.

'So,' Mike continued, 'for today's mystery tour, are you taking your bike or riding with me?' Much as he knew she liked her own ride, right now he'd rather have her close to him. She obviously felt the same.

'I'm definitely riding with you. Where are we going?'

'We're going house-hunting. I have a place I want you to see.'

'On Boxing Day?' said Tracy, disbelief in her voice.

'The estate agent's a friend, so he's doing me a favour. The house is vacant already, so he's trusting me with the keys — it means he can spend time with his family, and all the Christmas Day leftovers!'

She looked at him quizzically. 'If you say so,' she replied as she climbed aboard.

He headed out of the village towards Sheffield, but turned north onto a narrow road. He slowed and turned down a cobbled lane. When he stopped, Tracy caught her breath.

'What do you think?' he asked, hoping she loved it as much as he did. 'It comes with three acres bordering the Peaks.' He held his breath.

'It's absolutely gorgeous. I can't imagine a more perfect house for you. Can we go inside?' she asked eagerly.

'Yup.' He pulled the key out of his jacket pocket and walked up to the front door, holding Tracy's hand in his, then stopped and turned to face her. It was time to broach the question that had been almost constantly on his mind for the past few days, ever since Tracy had walked back into his bookshop and turned his world upside down.

'I love you,' he said, gazing directly into her eyes as he dropped to one knee in front of her. 'Marry me, Tracy. When I thought you were going to leave me, I was terrified. I need you with me, now and always. You're the missing part of my soul.'

She looked down and smiled at him, her heart overflowing with happiness. 'I love you, Mike. When I came home, I didn't think this would be my turn for a happily-ever-after. Yes, I'll marry you.'

Standing up, he put the key in the lock and opened the door, and then he picked her up and carried her over the threshold to a pile of pillows and blankets laid out on the floor in front of the stone fireplace. A bottle of wine sat in an ice bucket; two glasses beside it waited to be filled.

'What . . . ?'

He looked at her. 'Will this do?'

She grinned at him and he had his answer.

* * *

They'd spent the morning looking around the house and its grounds, and were now full from the picnic Brenda had prepared for them. As they lay together curled up in front of the fire Mike had lit to take the chill off the cold December day, Tracy turned to him and said, 'Favour from the estate agent, my foot! You're buying this house, aren't you?'

Mike laughed. 'I already have. I was sure you'd love it as much as I do. I've said it before — kindred spirits.' Her eyes shone as Mike continued. 'And that makes us even! Now, let me show you what I think of your decision to stay in Eyam with me.'

He rained kisses along her face, down the side of her neck. She leaned forward, kissing him back, and snuggled into his arms — the place he wanted her to stay for the rest of their lives.

He smiled. As G.L. O'Michael might say, life is an adventure, and theirs was just beginning.

THE END